Villa Fair

Villa Fair

stories by

Bernadette Dyer

Porcepic Books
an imprint of

Beach Holme Publishing
Vancouver

This book is published by Beach Holme Publishing, 226-2040 West 12th Avenue, Vancouver, B.C. V6J 2G2. This is a Porcepic Book.

The publisher gratefully acknowledges the financial support of the Canada Council for the Arts and of the British Columbia Arts Council. The publisher also acknowledges the financial assistance received from the Government of Canada through the Book Publishing Industry Development Program (BPIDP) for its publishing activities.

The Canada Council | Le Conseil des Arts
for the Arts | du Canada

BRITISH
COLUMBIA
ARTS COUNCIL
Supported by the Province of British Columbia

Editor: Michael Carroll
Production and Design: Jen Hamilton
Cover Art: *The Ruin* by Barrington Watson, 1987. 40" x 60", oil on canvas. Collection of the Orange Park Trust, Yallahs, St. Thomas, Jamaica. Used with the permission of the artist.
Author Photograph: Neil Davis

Printed and bound in Canada by Houghton Boston

Canadian Cataloguing in Publication Data

Dyer, Bernadette.
  Villa Fair

  "A Porcepic book."
  ISBN 0-88878-410-4

  I. Title.
PS8557.Y47V54 2000   C813'.54   C00-910659-6
PR9199.3.D95V54 2000

*Dedicated with love as a memorial to my mother,
the late Irene A. Gabay, who loved "Six Little Sparrows";
and to my nephew, the late Christopher Andrew Gabay,
who loved "Remembering Serge." And also to my brother,
David Anthony Gabay, who loves all of my stories.*

Contents

Acknowledgements

I would like to thank the various members of our multi-ethnic family: the Gabays, the Dyers, the Sweeneys, the Yamadas, the DiPronios, the Lyns, the Williamses, and the Phillipses for believing in me.

Thanks also to the following people for believing in my work: Carol Barbour, Lidia Colella, Mary Profiti, Diana Fitzgerald Bryden, William Beeton, W. Elaine Rodrigues, Jennifer Woolcock Schwartz, George Elliott Clarke, Paul Schwartz, Brian Smyth, Anne F. Walker, Lynn Crosbie, Hazelle Palmer, Ian Duff, Nalo Hopkinson, Rita Cox, Cheryl Phillips and, especially, Joy Gugeler, who saw something worth publishing, and Michael Carroll, my editor.

Special thanks to Nadine Gabay, who regularly read my work, and to Jorge Muniz Gomez for inspiring it. Thanks, too, to Belinda Wong for relentlessly typing my manuscripts.

And, finally, thanks to David, Shannon, and Rory for allowing me the time to work on the collection.

"Six Little Sparrows" was originally published in *Diva* in 1990. "An African Out in the Cold" was originally published in a slightly different version in *The Canadian Messenger* in 1991. "Ackee Night in Canada" was originally published in a slightly different version in *Authors Literary Magazine* in 1995.

Ackee Night in Canada

*E*veryone has some kind of addiction. I'm no different. Mine is my relationship with Dave. I allow him to consume me, though I know I might be better off exorcising him from my life. Initially I was attracted to him because he was so different and allowed me glimpses of another perspective on reality. But I am weary now and long for freedom in body and spirit. As for Dave, he's forever threatening to leave the city. He has this dream of heading out west. He feels things will go better for him there. He doesn't mention the fact that his old school friend, Nino Giovanelli, lives out there, or that Nino is now married and on welfare doing a little art work on the side. No, Dave likes to think that when he gets there things will fall into place, that he'll find a suitable room. One that isn't dusty or wanting for heat in the winter. One where his single bed won't squeak at the slightest touch. One where the noises from passing traffic won't overpower him. And one where, if there are people downstairs, they'll be good people and considerate, too, not like the ones where he is now, who are out to get him.

Dave isn't that fond of people; he likes being alone. Meditation is what he calls it. He spends his mornings in the park, thinking and assuming postures. On more than one occasion he's been approached by gays. Dave hates being bothered, especially by gays. Can he help it if he's lithe of frame and attractive? Heck, he's thirty-eight with the body of a twenty-one-year-old.

By afternoon he's exhausted but spends what's left of his energy practising on his bass guitar. He plays well but doesn't accept compliments easily. Dave is a perfectionist. He spends most evenings playing in dives around Toronto in a band called the Saltys. He despises all the band members, calls them assholes, and hates having to jam with strangers who always insist on using his equipment. "Why the heck," he says, "do I continually fall into the trap of thinking I have to be Mr. Nice Guy to these jerks?" He values isolation the way some people value possessions, and you dare not call him when he wants to be alone. If you do, he won't be rude outright. Instead he'll hardly say a word, speak monotonously, and practically slice you off the phone with his silences.

He enjoys a good feed, though, and can handle the spices in West Indian and East Indian cooking. He swears he's a vegetarian, but hasn't been known to refuse a good serving of meat. He heaps his plate at each meal as though it were his last, and without fail can find something or other wrong: too much salt, too little gravy, not enough potatoes, et cetera. He's one strange dude. You constantly get the feeling that if you were to push all the right buttons to please Dave, then he might stay in your life, and he might find it in his heart to reciprocate affection.

But then, with almost no warning, he'll pull what I call his St. Francis thing. He feels that people should have only the barest of possessions and live lives that are spare. Then, in the same breath, he'll reveal that if he had money, he'd have the right and might to live the sort of life he dreams of. He buys lottery tickets in the hope they'll take him off welfare and allow him to buy a new bass guitar, not like the one he has now but like that old black one he shouldn't have traded ten years ago. He would like a good flute, too. But never mind new clothes. He can manage with what little he already has. He would definitely get a haircut, though, because it might give him a better shot at meeting interesting women. He would also like tools. It has been too long now that he's been wanting tools to practise his cabinet-making. Manpower put him through a course fraught with frustration and assholes. But he came out clean in the end, producing three or four fine pieces of furniture.

There are times when I wonder if I had known Dave's track record whether I would have let him into my heart. A heart he handles as he would a meal, constantly searching for that telltale fault, that might-have-been, that if-your-custards-were-thicker-I-might-have-stayed sort of thing. For someone who wasn't supposed to be staying, Dave has stuck around for a long time. Ten years have come and gone, and he's still in danger of leaving. He still manages to wrench my heart with talk of getting up and going, and no amount of good cooking, good loving, or just plain goodness will persuade him to stay.

When I first saw him, he was as lean as he is today, with the same stained teeth I had attributed to tobacco but have since discovered is from all the tea drinking he does. He drinks six or more cups a day, a habit he acquired from having been born in Scotland where, whenever it got cold, which was most of the time, he was always reaching for a hot drink.

Dave once had nose surgery to improve his breathing. No, it wasn't by choice. His doctor told him the air passages were blocked in his nostrils because they were underdeveloped. But Dave swears it's dust that caused the problem, plus improper diet. He feels his doctor's a quack, and insists he's going to sue the guy for violating his nose. Trust me, there's nothing wrong with Dave's nose, not now, anyway.

"Sylvie," he says to me, "check my profile. Does my nose look crooked or anything?"

"No, Dave, it doesn't."

"It's got to. It doesn't feel right."

"Get a grip, Dave. Your nose is fine."

"Maybe I should be eating more green veggies and sunflower seeds. The vitamin content is quite high. It's gotta be good for healing and stuff."

It's as if Dave needs this nose thing to talk about all the time.

"You know, Sylvie, all the dust in my room is getting into my nose. I'm going to have to spend a week disinfecting the walls and floor."

"Sure, Dave."

"Hey, you weren't the one who had to have surgery."

He swears I should have known he was coming into my life. Swears I shouldn't have got married or had my three kids, even though all that happened long before I met him. And he wasn't joking when he said I should have seen him coming.

Sometimes he makes me feel guilty about owning a home; it's the St. Francis thing with him. Looking almost Christ-like with his beard and longish hair, he insists we should all live as frugally as possible.

"When I first saw your paintings," he often says, "I was blown away by the way you paint eyes. All those eyes seem to jump out of the canvas and follow you from room to room. It's freaky." Sometimes Dave is as innocent as a child, and it's at those times that the room seems to be filled with his beauty, and tears spring to my eyes. "You are one talented mother," he says, embarrassing me.

Quite often I steer Dave into the kitchen and cut him a slice of cornbread. It's his favourite, and it isn't something his granny used to make back in Scotland. It's uniquely mine.

"Love your baking," he always tells me, hunger lighting up his hazel eyes.

"What's for dinner?" he asks now. And I think, God, I wish I could come up with the right combination, that single ingredient, that one thing that will make him stay and never leave me.

I decide on ackee and cod; it's Jamaican like me. Ackee is a vegetable, delicious but potent, and poisonous if eaten unripe. It is fabulous with Canadian cod, and it's extra-fast to prepare. Dave will like it. I am outwardly calm, but my heart turns cartwheels.

Dave leans over the pot. "This will hit the spot," he says, and I hope he never realizes what hit him when the unripe ackees I have used kick in.

Man Man

*N*o one knew the plantation as well as ten-year-old Man Man Jefferson, for he walked all of its forty acres daily and had done so for years. He knew the old plantation house that stood on the hill overlooking banana, coconut, and citrus groves had been built during the time of slavery, and though not many people remembered those days, he certainly did.

Man Man enjoyed the peace and tranquillity of the garden in front of the house. He admired the roses that climbed on trellises in sprays of red, yellow, and pink, flowers that lost precious petals in the noonday tropical sun. Man Man imagined that was what snow must look like in foreign lands. He had never travelled and had never even been inside the plantation house, choosing to remain a fair distance from it, as he had been told to do a long time ago.

For the better part of each day, Man Man would meander down the steep incline, following ancient pathways through fields and groves until he came to where the air was heavy with salt and the land kissed the sea. He wasted no time chasing dragonflies as other children did, and was not distracted by bird song, for only the sea called him. The sea knew his supple black skin, knew his meagre frame and how easily he moved in and out of the water, and it was beside its shores that he once left a bundle of his best clothes and never reclaimed them. Other dark-skinned urchins like himself congregated at the seawall. And even now they spoke of him and imitated what he had done as they climbed nude up the jutting rocks, their eyes as wide as copper pennies as they hurled themselves into the swirling waters below, shivering, and knowing that not all of them would return unscathed.

Then one day a huge steamship came into port, and if Man Man had been with the other boys, he would have seen it, but he was up at the house worrying the chickens in the pens. He liked to hear them squawk as he ruffled their feathers, and loved to imitate their clucking. Had Man Man been at the beach, though, he would have seen when Geraldine Belmont, the new bride, arrived from England, which was far across the ocean.

Being up at the house, Man Man only saw young fair-haired William Belmont, the landowner dressed in his Sunday best, cross the yard, mount his dark bronze horse, Bonny King, and embark on a mission down the hill. Later, because he was walking the forty acres, Man Man missed the return of the lovers to the plantation house, missed seeing the red-gold hair of Geraldine Belmont glint in the hot sun. He missed seeing her eyes as deep and blue as the ocean, her smile as all-encompassing as the surrounding vistas. Had Man Man been there he might have seen William Belmont swell with zest as he swept his bride over the threshold, laughing as they entered the house where all the servants lined up to receive them. There was old Miriam, the brown-skinned cook with dimples in her faded cheeks, and stockings rolled up at her knees; Solomon, the curly-haired, dusky-skinned teenage houseboy who was rumoured to be a Belmont himself; Joseph, the old faithful black gardener who coaxed roses to bloom in the tropical surroundings; and, last of all, Sheba, the housemaid and assistant cook, with flaming kinky red hair and copper skin, wearing a surly look on her pretty face, realizing perhaps that her embraces were being replaced.

Man Man did not see the new bride until a week after her arrival. He had been out back admiring new roses Joseph had put in, blood-red flowers with petals as smooth as a velvet dress Man Man's own mother had once worn. So engrossed was he that he was quite unaware when Geraldine came up to him.

"Do you like roses?" she asked, her soft English voice foreign to his ears, her pale complexion and eyes momentarily startling him. He tried to wrap his tongue around words, but nothing would come out, so he turned his head away shyly. Geraldine sensed his confusion and invited him inside. "Come," she said, "have a drink of juice or something."

But Man Man only shook his head, endearing himself to her as he moved aside in his shabby clothes and bare feet.

"Poor thing," she said out loud, following him with her eyes before she noticed the long line of banana groves that snaked up the hillside for miles behind the house.

"It's dreadfully dark there," she said, as if warning him, nodding toward the silent trees. "Has there ever been any danger of robbers hiding in there?"

Man Man did not answer, though he had seen many things, seen lanterns weave up the hillside to the house, heard when all hell broke loose, and Miss Constance, a former landowner, was raped, beaten, and driven mad, then confined to a nursing home. The same Miss Constance who had once been kind to him. He had seen death, too. He had watched it visit the old house again and again, and he had witnessed both good and bad. He saw Sheba bury a girl child beneath the spreading banyan tree, and he had heard old Miriam thanking the Lord for all the good she was able to do for others through her long years. But Man Man said nothing as he walked away, head down and silent.

When Geraldine went into the house and asked Miriam about the boy, she failed to get any clues to his identity. It was almost as though Man Man did not exist, for Miriam never spoke of the many Christmases she had left small food packages for him on the back steps, and she made no mention of the bundle of antique clothes found at the seawall and passed down by family through generations, or how her heart had kept hoping and hoping.

Geraldine next approached Joseph the gardener, but he only wagged his tired old head and mumbled, "Some things are best left well enough alone. The boy has been here for a long time." From what little she could gather, Geraldine learned that the boy was a loner and that he was seen mostly on Friday nights when the plantation held a gathering for storytelling and revelry, for one or two regulars had seen him there.

There was a full moon on the night of the gathering, and all the servants, field hands, and labourers from other plantations came. Before the stories started, they built a roaring fire and passed around foaming tin cups of cane juice and rum. Geraldine watched from indoors, impatient to join in, but was gently restrained by William's kisses as he explained that her presence would ruin the spontaneity of the event. She watched and listened from the darkened dining-room window, well aware of all the comings and goings of mothers, fathers, children, and old folks, and the young men whose backs were weary from lifting and loading, and the full-lipped young women who invited their kisses.

Then, at last, Man Man came as silent as a shadow. He kept

well apart from the others, blending in with the dark, his copper eyes bright with listening. Geraldine wondered if he was lonely. He seemed an outcast, sitting there with no arms encircling him, no broad lap for him to snuggle in.

It was long into the evening before the stories ended and the revelry wound down, and William Belmont was fast asleep, but not Geraldine. When the people began to disperse, she raced through the darkened house and exited by the servants' quarters. She searched out Man Man from the crowd and, finding him, kept her eyes on him. Startled by the sounds of crickets and frogs and the yapping of dogs in the distance, however, she almost collided with old Joseph, who was hobbling home.

"Sorry, Joseph," she said, trying to catch her breath. "Please come with me!" She sounded so urgent that Joseph obliged, tottering after her into the retreating moonlight.

"It's late, ma'am," Joseph mumbled. "Your husband will be missing you."

But Geraldine Belmont was not to be deterred. Together they followed the boy from a safe distance, dodging in and out of foliage even as he wandered into the forbidding banana grove.

"Let him be, ma'am," Joseph whispered. "He knows the land like the back of his hand."

But Geraldine ignored his words, her attention firmly fixed on the clearing she now saw ahead. In the full moonlight Man Man paused and wearily bowed his small head, his hair silver in the light. Then, without warning, the moonlight retreated, and Man Man, too, was no longer there! No twig snapped to betray his presence, no animal or insect called, there was no movement in the brush, only the dark night yawning.

Geraldine, and old Joseph moving as fast as he could, hurried into the clearing, eyes wild with searching out the boy. But only a small boulder stood sentry, a stone field marker perhaps from the old days. Geraldine saw that there were words carved into its smooth surface, words old Joseph could not read, words older than him. She bent low and, with trembling lips, read the inscription out loud:

>Here lies Man Man Jefferson
>Aged 10 years
>Who departed this life on May 26 by drowning
>In the year of Our Lord 1806
>May he rest in peace.

Six Little Sparrows

I first saw them on a spring morning, the kind of day when sunbeams slant into windows creating unforgettable images. On such a morning they arrived, babbling happily while hanging on to their mother's side. The children laughed at the sunshine, eyes filled with honesty and adoration.

What bright colours they all wore—red, blue, lime-green! Everyone else paled in comparison, and I sat in drabness in a library of dark, dusty books that cried out for a drop of sunlight to enhance their true majesty. For me, it seemed the children's hues were the only lustre added to my day.

They must have been from Pakistan originally, for the cut of their clothes was definitely Eastern. It's funny, but now that I think of it, I could almost see the lands of the East in their pale grey-green eyes. None of them was as dark as other Pakistanis I had met. In fact, they seemed light-skinned. All the children had inherited the mother's classic beauty. Her face was a picture of serenity, though a certain softness betrayed her youth.

Sitting at my charge-out desk, I had a good view of them, and I'd watch as their little feet carried them across the grass, never straying far from the watchful eye of the mother. There was a mystical bond here, I thought. It was hard to keep my eyes off them, though library work was most demanding. The little family perhaps had no garden or sun porch, so they used the parkette beside the library as such, but they were never loud or destructive.

The children's voices tinkled like small bells, while their brown heads bobbed in the wind and the sun itself seemed to enjoy catching startling colours in their hair: unearthly reds, burnt auburns, browns, and blacks. It became quite a diversion to watch the "six little sparrows," as I called them, setting up residence outside the window, and mother sparrow keeping her vigil. On grey days they still came, all wearing sweaters much too small or thin. But they still wore sunshine-warm smiles on their faces. It was as though they had a pact with nature to chase away the rain. Nonetheless, rain did come, and the "sparrows" never appeared on such days.

Theirs was a ritual one could easily get accustomed to. They arrived in the morning and left in the evening, and after they were gone, I was suddenly aware of a certain stillness, for the music of their high-pitched chirping no longer drifted through the window.

One day the youngest of them, "the baby," climbed through the open library window. Since the upper edge of the book-shelves was in line with the windowsill, that put her right on top of them. She sat quite prettily in her salmon silks, not even aware of the danger. When the mother noticed the baby missing, she drew her remaining "sparrows" to her and quickly made her way into the library.

I knew by instinct that it was the first time any of them had been inside such a building. Immediately I was reminded of caged birds as the bright eyes of the children peered into every nook and cranny while expressing delight at the books. But through it all, I also sensed fear, for they must have felt we would keep them there, using the enticement of the books as bait.

The mother tenderly gathered her baby into the softness of her silken robes, and at the same time motioned to the others to stay close. They didn't speak a word of English, but they needed no language to express the love between them. It was as if a golden light followed them.

The eldest of the children was a boy about nine years old. He was the only one who looked us in the eye and smiled. His smile brought light into our dark room, and his shiny eyes expressed such a longing that we somehow knew that if any of the "sparrows" were to come back, it would be him. And when he turned away with the rest of them on his sandaled feet, we felt cheated of that smile.

Many days passed, and I found myself anticipating the arrival of "my family of sparrows." I heard their high-pitched cries as I carried out routine tasks that took on a certain dullness in contrast to the joy and light of the little family.

The oldest boy, bolder now, had started to peer in at the windows. The lure of the books became irresistible, and his smile now held a hint of sadness. Was he no longer satisfied with running and playing in the grass?

Spring changed to summer and still they came. Now they shared their meagre lunches with the birds. The mother's sweetness seemed to attract these gentle creatures, for they fearlessly ate from her bare hands. The children, too, had the same sweetness, and the sunlight appeared to dance to the sound of their happy voices.

What a summer that was! The summer of my sparrows. It was the season of one family spreading love beyond itself. I can sometimes see them in my mind as though they were still there. But since the mother mostly kept her back to the window, I didn't realize that, amid the love and laughter, sadness had crept into her grey-green eyes. If only I had known what was to come, then perhaps I might have been prepared, but alas, I was not.

One day, when autumn finally came, a class from the local school visited the library. I was delighted to see that the eldest "little sparrow" was in that class. He still spoke no English, but his eager eyes embraced every book, and he turned pages with such reverence that it made my heart nearly burst with joy.

He was allowed only two books, but I let him have four, for such was the newfound delight of this child. Though it was autumn, I noticed his feet were still sandaled. His bright eyes still teased sunbeams to play in his hair, but I could almost feel the shiver in his bones.

It was late fall before I realized I had missed the daily visits of the little family. It was much too cold for sitting outdoors in summer clothes. I longed to hear their bell-like laughter and to see sunbeams gambol on their golden cheeks. But it was not to be. Though I searched for them, they were nowhere to be found. I still feel that year must have been the coldest winter of all, for they had taken the sun with them.

Winter was quite long and the loveliness of the little family slipped to the back of my memory. But then came spring. Once again I heard the chirping of the voices as bell-like sounds filled the air. Gazing up at the window, I expected to see my "sparrows" back, just the way it had always been. But they weren't there! I felt an urgency to find them. Leaving my desk, I went outside.

It was the sort of day when sunshine slanted into windows and created unforgettable images. The crocuses were up, and small green things pushed themselves out of the soil. Then, there in front of me, was the most amazing sight! A sparrow and her six little chicks were resting by the window. Their high, happy cries could be heard above the passing traffic.

At the sound of my approach, the mother sparrow turned her grey-green eyes toward the sky, and in a moment she and her six little charges were on the wing and their silhouettes etched against the blue sky.

Six Little Sparrows

Years later, by a roundabout route, I was told that my little family had returned to Pakistan unexpectedly. But somehow I knew they had said goodbye, and that wherever they are, the "six little sparrows" are safe with their mother, and the memory of them is safe with me.

Close the Blue Door

*M*y grandfather told me I was fathered by a merman. He
said he had always lived beside the Rio Conde and that
he believed in spirits and knew the river's moods. During the
course of his life, he had seen the river swell dangerously and
become deadly many times. He had known its silences and had
heard the raucous quarrelling of its currents when the spirits
were angry. When the river became strong enough to sweep
away houses, full-grown trees, animals, and humans, he
became truly afraid. But more than anything else, he was in awe
of the merpeople because he knew they occasionally mated
with humans.

Grandfather said that his fair-skinned daughter, Saville, who
was my mother, was chosen by the river's merpeople from the
moment of her birth, for she was born with a thin membrane over
her face, which was a true sign of the merpeople's ownership.

That was why when she was a baby he took her down to the river to play in the shallows among the rocks and ferns, where she would delight in the little fish that came to nibble her small pink toes. Grandfather would sprinkle water gently on top of her head and ask the river spirits to spare her from drowning. Then he would brush her small feet with soft, dry sand, beseeching the spirits to keep her always on solid ground. My grandfather was a man who believed in nature spirits, and he never broke bread without giving thanks. He said that spirits existed on the Earth to carry out the work of the Lord in heaven.

Saville was very much like my grandfather in appearance. For she, too, was fair and considered "red," which in our part of the island referred to blacks who were so light-skinned they appeared Caucasian. My grandmother, on the other hand, was as dark as the skin of a naseberry, and her hair as black as star-apple seeds. There was an unmistakable bond between Saville and my grandfather; perhaps that was why her first word was "Da" and her first eager steps were taken toward him.

My grandparents were as dirt-poor as all the other riverside dwellers who lived in houses little better than shanties. They survived on the daily catch, sweet potatoes, cassavas and, occasionally, rice. My grandmother made a small living selling cassavas as a roadside vendor along the asphalt road that ran near the river.

As Saville grew older, she gazed down that road and wondered about the great distances it covered, and the marvels that lay beyond the horizon. She would light her kerosene lamp at night and give thanks for all those at home, never forgetting to ask the fire spirits to spare her family, always praying they would not follow the evils that surely existed along the road.

Saville did not attend school. My grandparents could not afford it, and besides they could not bear to be apart from her, for the school was many miles down that same road. Instead, Grandfather took her to see the mirrorlike water of the river on clear, still days, and in the evenings they would witness the return of the gaunt black fishermen who made a slender living from the sea.

My mother learned the ways of survival, never wanting more than she was given, but often she would fall into feverish trances, listening to the river's rhythms and murmurings. When Grandfather saw her like that, he would become solemn and sad, his voice as soft as a whisper.

"Don't listen to the voices of the merpeople," he would warn. "They will try to lure you away and you will never see us again."

Hearing his words, Saville would cry great tears and promise never to leave him.

"And always remember to close the blue door at night," he would insist, "for it is our only door that looks out over the river, and the merpeople will climb up the rocky riverbank and come in through it into the house to take you away."

One languid afternoon when Saville was fifteen she went down to the river as usual with Grandfather. He fell into a fitful sleep in the hot sun as he sat against a large boulder. In her loneliness for his company, Saville heard a strange whistle, unlike any she had heard before. She stepped over the sharp rocks, leaving her father's side, following the seductive whistling for more than a mile, almost to the mouth of the river. Coming upon a large moss-encrusted cave, reputed to be the abode of the merpeople, Saville thought nothing of it. Fearless, she crouched beneath overhanging vines and parted thick green river rushes, paying no heed to her father's warnings as she entered the cave.

When she returned to her father, he was only just waking from his sleep, brushing ferns and lily pollen from his hair. As his watery eyes fell on Saville, he sensed that something about her was not the same, but he was still too heavy with sleep to think exactly what it was. Soon the pleasant burble of the river assured him that all was well.

Saville took to seeking out the cave each time her father fell asleep on the riverbank. It was as though the river itself had consumed her, for she burned with a mysterious passion no longer satisfied with mere river murmurings.

But one day, on waking, Grandfather found her missing. His heart almost failed, he could hardly breathe, and a great pain lodged in his breast as his eyes misted with tears. He called out in terror to the river spirits, asking them to tell him where Saville was. Hearing no reply, he willed himself strength to climb over the rocks and weave a path through the ferns and rushes. More than once he thought he saw the wet outline of other footprints on the stones. When he came upon the forbidden cave, his heart filled with fear. "Saville!" he cried out, half hoping for no answer. Then, suddenly, he was deafened by the sound of a great thundering splash, and the thought of Saville among the merpeople filled him with great sorrow.

His trepidation vanished when Saville joyfully ran from the cave into his weary arms. He held her for a long time and cried freely. "We have to remember to close the blue door tonight," he told her.

After that, Saville took to her mother's company, becoming solemn and silent, reminding her father of the river with its ever-changing moods as she fell into household tasks. She no longer visited the river, though at night she found herself compelled to leave the blue door open after her parents fell asleep, and she would hear the strange whistling and the soothing stroke of the river against the shore. Her nights became dreamless, yet it seemed to her that she slept in the very arms of the dark river, for she felt its breath hot upon her cheeks, felt its currents and its foam penetrate her, felt its tongue warm against her flesh.

Grandfather was the first to notice Saville's changes. His daughter grew rosy, her lean frame straining to form new proportions as her thin, pale cheeks and her belly, month after month, blossomed like flowers.

"She is having a baby!" Grandmother exclaimed one morning.

"Our poor child is having a baby!"

"I should have put a stop to it!" Grandfather thundered. "I should have boarded up that damn door! It is the work of the merpeople. She has been in their cave!"

By the time I was born, Saville no longer went near the river. Instead, she brooded indoors, always sitting with me in her arms by the blue door. Her eyes looked inward as streams flowed from them, baptizing me in river tears. And a wall grew up between her and her parents, surrounding them in loneliness.

Early one morning my mother jumped off a wooden bridge that spanned the widest point of the river and drowned herself. The river dwellers said she had returned to the merman in the river.

When I was growing up, a free government school opened near our settlement. I walked alone there, since both my grandparents had grown feeble. At the school I was called the River Child, though my true name was Lily, named for the flower that dots the meandering river. One day, when I was fourteen, I saw an old East Indian woman as I was returning home from school. She was bent under the weight of a bundle of sticks that she carried. Her eyes shone like coals and her wrinkled skin was almost translucent. My grandfather would have thought she was a fairy, but I knew she was human, being subject to her long, steady gaze.

"Good evening, child," she said, revealing discoloured teeth. A rope of grey-black hair was swung over her shoulder.

"Good evening," I replied, noticing her shaggy brows and unsteady hand. "Let me help you with your load."

She smiled, then painfully lowered the bundle to the ground, redistributed it, and gave me a load of my own. "Thank you," she rasped like a death rattle. "What is your name, child?"

"It's Lily."

"You are from the river settlement?"

"Yes."

"Well, I will tell you something I have told no one before."

Bearing our heavy burdens, we walked side by side in silence for miles, even as the sun dipped low in the sky and bathed the trees and shrubs in gold.

"It will be too late for you to walk back alone," the old woman finally said. "You will have to stay the night. I will walk with you in the morning."

My heart sank, for I had never been away from my grandparents for even a night, and I was fearful for them and for my missing them. We trudged on through bush and briar until at last we approached a small zinc house.

"Come inside," the old woman said. "Leave your sticks by the door." We entered the dirt-floor shack and she said, "So you are called Lily. It is a good name for someone as light-skinned as you, and look how your hair is long and dark. You could practically pass for a Coolie Indian like me. My husband and son were also Indian. But my husband, Vikram, was a heavy drinker and him beat us up all the time for no reason. And even when I love him, him beat me, anyway. That is why my son, Rajiv, run away. Rest your feet, girl. Sit in this chair. Is the only one I have. Let me just squat on this old pan and I will tell you all about him. My husband is dead now, choked on him vomit one night, and now I am alone. When I was young, people knew me as Gaitree Ladrin, but these days I am called Coolie Old Woman."

She grinned. "I loved my son so much. I spoiled him with love, for we had nothing else to give him. Look at me now, old and withered. You must find it hard to think of me as a beauty, but people say that is what I was. But, Lily, I am straying from the story. Is what we old people do. As I said before, Rajiv's father's drinking drove my son away. When him was seventeen, him found a cave down by the Rio Conde. Him did not know that cave was the place black people say is the merpeople's house, for we Coolies did not really mix with blacks. It was a godforsaken place a long way from here. But him did not tell me all I tell you.

Him left a diary, which I, an uneducated woman, could not read. It is only through the goodness of the priest who read it for me that I know the story.

"Don't fall asleep in the chair, Lily. You have to listen, so others will know. Rajiv write in the book that one day him saw a beautiful young girl along the riverbank. She was very light-skinned, with hair the colour of honey. Him watched her daily while hiding behind the rocks. Then one day Rajiv whistle a tune on a tin flute, and she followed the sound as him led her away from a sleeping old man. Him dodge behind rock after rock, and she follow him right to the cave where him was living. The girl was a strange one. Him said she did not stop him hugs or kisses. And when him said, 'Take your clothes off,' she did. Rajiv said they met every chance they could, and him even manage to find her house among the shacks beside the river in the same settlement you are from. Him enter her room at night through a blue door, and though the girl lay with him night after night, Rajiv said him feel like she did not even know him was there.

"My son and me were close. And I know him had big dreams, because him had gone to school and had learning. Him dreamed of following the asphalt road to the city to make something of himself, and one night him did follow that road. Him quickly packed a few things by moonlight, so him daddy would not know. And with a kiss on my cheek as sharp as a hen's peck, him gone. That night, Lily, Rajiv Ladrin was killed on the asphalt road, struck down by a market truck, and the driver get off, 'cause him say him not see Rajiv in the dark. And now I will never see my son again."

I turned my eyes away from the old woman as she tucked me in for the night in a bed of rags that at one time might have been her son's. I longed to dream of my grandparents, even as she caught me in her fierce black-eyed gaze.

"I had to tell someone," she said. "For my son was beautiful, so very beautiful."

Peaches and Creame

*I*n Toronto, not far from the corner of College Street and Euclid Avenue, stands Fred's Haberdashery. It is considered a prime location since business picked up on that strip of College with the opening of trendy cafés, bars, and bookshops.

Two middle-aged sisters, Betty and Lolly Martin, inherited the haberdashery from their long-deceased father, Fred. The business kept them fairly active, but these days they were rarely in the store and considered themselves semiretired. However, the day-to-day operation was relegated to their two younger energetic cousins, Peaches and Vivian Salmon.

Betty, the eldest of the two semiretired sisters, was fifty-five, and was widowed due to an unfortunate house fire in the West Indies when she was twenty-six. She never remarried, and although bearing no physical scars, her carefree outlook on life evaporated in that fire and she became methodical and serious-minded.

Lolly, the younger sister, at fifty, had a zest for life. It was she who ran the internal operations of the business and who saw to it that their records balanced. Unlike her sister, she never married. Their father used to say she was spoiled, having been given too many opportunities. As a young woman, she went to business college, and although a popular student with her good looks and hazel eyes, she had never met Mr. Right. Through the years her looks mellowed, and her lush, dark hair streaked with silver was held back severely in a broad silver clasp that strained under the weight of her heavy hair.

Stores such as theirs were not uncommon in the neighbourhood, nor was it unusual that women ran the whole operation; what was unusual in that Italian-Portuguese stronghold of the city was that these women were black.

Vivian, their twenty-five-year-old cousin, was thin, tall, dark, and distinctive, with a full crop of dreadlocks. She was a former art student and instinctively knew how to adorn herself well. On her, everything looked right—the cross-and-skull earrings, the baggy tops, and the long black skirts split up the sides to her knees.

On the other hand, Peaches, her twenty-one-year-old sister, was plain and slightly overweight, a problem that persisted in spite of all her daily physical work. Starting most mornings at 6:30, she set up daily displays, checked and organized stock, and strategically placed plastic bins of merchandise in front of the store to attract passersby. Life for her was a steady stream of work and more work.

One afternoon Peaches, who enjoyed being outside, was in front of the store, keeping an eye on the well-stocked bins. She was never one to think about her appearance. If she had looked into a mirror, she would have seen her windblown hair wild with tangles like a lion's mane around her face. But she was otherwise a good observer and was alert when a cyclist pulled up and began to rifle through the bins. Peaches kept her eyes on him. She was extra-vigilant since he had a bicycle, which made for a quick getaway if he was a thief.

The cyclist lingered over housewares, socks, and then gloves. Peaches almost froze when a low whistle escaped his throat and she saw he was holding up an egg cup. "Haven't used one of these in years," he said. "I'll have to get one." Peaches glanced sideways at him; his delight was infectious. "And look, you have Ovaltine biscuits!"

Peaches tugged at her unruly hair and looked at him more closely. As far as she was concerned, egg cups were useless and Ovaltine biscuits were no big deal. What was he up to? Then she noticed the small dimple in his cheek and saw that the curly blond hair spilling out from under his cycling helmet made him look almost roguish as delight shone in his steel-grey eyes.

By the time he left the store some fifteen minutes later, the cyclist had purchased enough items to fill his large knapsack. On departure he touched his hand to his helmet, then headed west on College.

No sooner had he left than Vivian, who was regularly on cash, hurried out, her long black skirt flapping in the wind, revealing a firm thigh. Grinning, she asked, "Did you see him? He was real nice."

"Well, I don't think we'll see him again," Peaches said. "He looked like he got everything he wanted."

"You right, girl. It was enough for an army." Both girls laughed, though each, in her own way, was still admiring the young man who didn't look a day older than Peaches.

A couple of days later Peaches, deep in surveillance outside the store, was taken aback when a bicycle pulled up beside her.

"Hi," the rider said, touching his helmet. It was the same young man.

"Hi," she replied sheepishly.

"Could use some more biscuits. I'll take a look inside, too, just to make sure I didn't miss anything."

Peaches's laugh was rich and deep, although she watched enviously as he stepped inside the store. But in less than ten minutes he was waving goodbye, and Vivian, unable to contain herself, was out of the store in a flash.

"Well, I don't know if is you or me he like 'cause he just bought a bunch of rubbish I sure he don't need, so he musta did come to see one of us."

Peaches grinned. "Is not me for sure. Must be you with your dreads and slit skirt."

"Ah, come on, girl, I'm not that hot, am I? Anyway, him sound English. You notice?"

"No, not really, 'cause him didn't really say much to me."

The next day the cyclist was back, but this time Peaches half expected him. However, Betty and Lolly were in the store on one of their visits and, as a result, Peaches thought it best not to have too much to do with the man. In spite of his cool reception, the cyclist poked his head in the doorway and greeted Vivian breezily, then began to browse. It was a good twenty minutes before he left. Peaches, stationed outside, had to wait for an opportunity to find out from Vivian what had happened inside.

"Did he say anything?" she asked.

"No, he just stared," Vivian replied. "But what could you expect with Lolly beside me taking stock? I couldn't say nothing, either." Both girls laughed. "Can you imagine what Lolly would say if she saw us drooling over this white man?"

"Well, not me," Peaches said. "I just curious. I don't drool."

After that the young man came every second day, and Vivian grew more confident that he came to see her. She began wearing more daring outfits to work, and her necklines plunged danger-ously, revealing ample cleavage. To Peaches, it looked as if Vivian was dressing for a part in some sort of game. But she herself quickly became tired of the whole thing, especially since it occurred to her that the young man, whom they discovered was called James Creame, couldn't really be smart at all, since he didn't even know that it wasn't wise to hang around the store when Betty and Lolly were there. But James took to having serious discussions with Lolly, and Peaches wondered if she was wrong about him, for they discussed everything from the price of mousetraps to communism in the Third World. With Betty he even proposed the possibility of opening a West Indian section in the store, something she had been thinking about for a long time. His ideas were well thought out, and it was clear his feet were firmly planted on the ground. Through it all, Vivian saw everything as James's ruse for coming to see her. She cared not a hoot for politics or animal traps, and she relished painting her lips and her lids a smoky brown while James looked on.

Peaches, still not knowing what to make of it all, concluded that James, by associating with them, was vicariously reliving memories of his early youth when he spent four years in Jamaica with his English parents on a sugarcane estate. He was ten back then, he said, and had seen much of the island and its people.

The usually sedate Betty regaled him with anecdotes from her youth, and Lolly spoke of fun-filled holidays by the sea. Peaches, however, was not the only one taking stock of things, for Betty, too, noticed a blossoming in the women around her. She saw that Peaches now kept her unkempt hair tidy. She saw Lolly rejuvenate. And as far as Vivian was concerned, she had never looked so attractive. Betty could swear that they were all looking into the store's full-length mirror more often. She herself harnessed her wayward stomach in a corset and set about pulling her slumping shoulders back to reveal her healthy chest. Smiles once more visited her lips, and she felt that all was right with the world, since James started coming to their store.

So it was somewhat of a surprise to Peaches when one Tuesday afternoon James didn't show up at the store. His classes at the University of Toronto were usually over by 12:30 on Tuesdays. Normally he would have had a spot of lunch at one of the local cafés before heading over to see them. She pretended that she thought nothing of it when Vivian remarked that James was late.

But that afternoon proved to be a busy one. Vivian found herself with a lineup at her cash register, and to make matters worse, the telephone started to ring.

"Peaches!" she shouted. "Can you get that?"

Peaches, ever vigilant, came racing into the store out of breath and grasped the receiver. "Hello, Fred's Haberdashery."

"It's me, Betty" came the soft reply.

"Are you coming to the store?"

Betty hesitated, as though taking a deep breath. "Brace yourself, girl. Something happen."

Peaches cocked the phone closer to her ear, her eyes wild with anticipation.

"What's going on?" Vivian hissed from the cash register.

"Is Betty and she trying to say something," Peaches whispered, raising a finger to her lips to silence Vivian.

"Are you still there?" Betty asked, sighing as though the weight of the world were upon her shoulders.

"Yes," Peaches replied, full of dread.

"Well, is Lolly this all about."

"What happened, Betty?"

"I don't know how to put this so it don't shock you, so I might as well be blunt. Lolly gone run away with James Creame. Them get married last night. She say she finally found Mr. Right."

Johns Lane

*T*he room I was in that day reeked of death. I had come to know its presence. It lingered in cracks in walls and in the floors, and it lived between the cool sheets of my grandfather's bed, where he lay waxen and cold, his thick, straight hair still dark in death pasted against his ivory skin. I could not take my eyes off him. He had been in my heart too long. I wanted to place my fingers on his cheeks to let him know I was there. But my grandmother, Popo Lini, stopped me. She paid her tribute in silence, and I had to follow her example.

Grandfather's room was small, dust particles floated in the air, and a dusky curtain at the window filtered the light. Grandmother was oblivious to the overpowering odour of the carbolic soap she used to scrub his wooden floors, and her nose did not twitch at the dettol-and-water mixture that washed down the walls. She was lost in thoughts and memories, and I had to be silent. I was ten, almost eleven, but I was not afraid, not like my older and younger sisters who kept their distance confined to their room. But I knew that like me, they, too, were remembering Grandfather's story. He had told it to us so many times, and we knew he probably never thought death would find him, never thought he would give in on his final breath, for he had raged with life and had bubbled over with dreams.

When he first came to Jamaica from China, my grandfather, Yuping Lee, had been a young man, bringing his young bride, Lini, with him. They were lucky enough to buy cheap cultivatable land in the west country, and fell into farming with enthusiasm. The couple planted and harvested crops of oranges, bananas, coconuts, and peppers; learned to follow the passage of birds to predict the weather; and rejoiced in rainy and dry seasons. They had been hard workers in China; Jamaica proved no different for them. But after a few years of working the farmland, Lini became pregnant and Grandfather decided to move to Kingston, Jamaica's capital city, since more opportunities for advancement existed there for their child. The birth of their daughter, Fiona, held them like a root to the island, and they resigned themselves to settling permanently, although they had at one time dreamed of returning to China.

The small run-down home they bought was in the downtown core of Kingston on Johns Lane, and it was that very building celebrating birth that was to become the house of death where my grandparents were to say goodbye to each other forever.

My grandmother, or Popo Lini as she preferred to be called, remained in that room of death for three days, neither eating nor sleeping, her eyes wide in disbelief, staring at nothing in particular. "Yuping, Yuping" were the only words that came from her throat, and the sound of hopelessness in her voice still haunts my memory. Who knows how long we would have remained in vigil in that sweltering room if our black neighbours, the Edwardses, had not come over to check on us? Mrs. Edwards, her husband, and their daughter, Barbara, who was my age, all came. Thanks to them, an undertaker was notified and our family was treated to a hot, nourishing meal, and even Popo Lini's refusal to eat was met with sympathetic, successful coaxing on the part of Mrs. Edwards.

"You have to eat for the sake of the grandchildren," she said. "They will need you more than ever now."

We were sadder, however, because our own mother was not there. She was not even in the city, for she had left us with Popo Lini and had gone to reside in Caracas, Venezuela. At times it was hard to remember my mother except through tears. I remembered her slim, cool hands, her long black hair, and her eyes that slanted like perfect almonds. To me, she was a bumble-bee forever flitting out of reach. How we missed her, though she offered no real explanation for leaving us behind. Still, I could not help but feel that it must have had something to do with the many "uncles" she used to introduce us to—uncles who were not even Chinese.

"Too many Chinese already in the family," she used to say. "Time for a change."

My father was Chinese from China. He had settled in Jamaica by way of Montreal, Canada, where some of his family lived. Father felt beaten by the weather there and could not accustom himself to its severity. He decided to relocate to the warm Caribbean, where he opened an import-export shop. There, he met my mother, who was at first his secretary, then his wife.

Papa was solitary and brimmed with loneliness. It kept him isolated and introspective, and were it not for Mama he would have returned to his homeland. He was not even aware that Barry Street, where we lived above the business, had begun to deteriorate. And he was equally unaware of the hordes of cock-roaches that infested our rooms, causing my sisters and I to stamp them to death with our hard-soled Bata shoes as a daily ritual. Papa certainly would not have approved.

But one memorable morning everything changed. Mama came into the room I shared with my sisters. She was pale, and her downcast eyes made her seem as fragile as a trembling leaf about to fall from a tree. I screwed up my eyes, pretending to sleep, fearful of what she had to say. My sisters, too, must have sensed something, for they huddled in tense silence against my rigid body. Little Katryn, who was four, hardly dared to breathe and Megan, who was thirteen, held both our hands under the covers, trembling.

"Papa gone back to China," Mama said.

Her words were to change forever the course of our future, and there was no stopping the flow of tears in the room that morning.

We did not go to school that morning. Mama did not seem to mind, not even when Megan complained of the stifling heat indoors and took Katryn to play outside on the busy Barry Street sidewalk. I did not want to play. I only wanted to lie in bed and think of Papa. Mama must have been eager to have us out of her hair, for as soon as the front door slammed, she was on the telephone with her best friend, Joyce Chen. Obviously she thought we had all left the house.

"Him gone," she said to Joyce breezily. "Him musta find out, so is only the children now is the worry, 'cause I have to find them a place to stay."

The conversation ended abruptly when my bedsprings let out a squeal as I turned over. I kept still valiantly after that whenever I heard Mama's footsteps head toward our room, and did my best to pretend to sleep. I must have been convincing, for I would always hear her footsteps retreat after a moment's pause.

Those were times when the weeks passed like years. Then, one afternoon, quite unexpectedly, an old, dishevelled black beggar everyone knew as Long John came to the business to see us. Mama spoke to him, and he informed her that he had urgent news for the family. She slipped him a few coins to learn that a cousin of hers, known to us as Mr. Tim, wanted to see us right away. "Why didn't he come himself?" I wondered out loud. But my question was not answered.

Mr. Tim ran a small grocery store on Orange Street, not far from our home. He was serving customers when Mama arrived with us in tow.

"So, why you send for us, Tim?" she asked, still clutching our hands.

"Is bad news," Mr. Tim replied gravely. "Him dead and buried already."

"Who dead?" Mama demanded, letting her hands fall to her sides.

"Your husband gone go dead in China. Them say it was suicide."

Mama reeled on the spot. Then, gathering strength, she leaned against the wooden counter for support. "How you know is true, Tim?"

"I know because Aunt Viki in Beijing send a telegram."

"So why nobody send me nothing?"

"Maybe because him did cut you off. Remember?"

Mama said we were never to mention Papa to her again.

Immediately after leaving Mr. Tim's, she dragged us across Kingston's congested streets, past the vendors selling whistles, fifes, and peanuts, past the market women, the cyclists, and the honking lines of vans, cars, and trucks. She looked neither left nor right in her haste and did not stop until we came to Johns Lane, a narrow, decaying street where pushcarts rumbled alongside us. Domino players had set up places on the pavement and games were in progress. I immediately noticed the stray dogs that yapped at one another as scantily dressed black children set paper boats afloat down a swift-moving gutter of debris. Mama stopped in front of one of the smaller houses; it was easy to see that it was falling into disrepair. I saw a pulse beat at Mama's throat, but at the time I did not know I was looking at the home of my grandparents. Mama stood on the veranda and knocked feebly. The door opened instantly. A small, ancient Chinese woman with swollen ankles, well-worn slippers, and wispy grey hair that barely covered her scalp stood there. Her face was a sea of wrinkles, as faded as the shift she wore. Recognizing Mama, she broke into a smile.

"Fiona!" she croaked, extending her thin, wrinkled hands to take us all in.

"Popo!" Mama said. "These are your *suin*."

The old woman, who was Mama's grandmother, our Tai Popo, smelled of garlic and coconut milk.

"This is your great-grandmother," Mama said. "She came from China to be with my mother when I was born. The two women babbled in what sounded to us like strange Chinese words before Tai Popo waved us inside.

"Come in, come in," she coaxed. "Not to worry. No dog to bite you. Lini! Lini!" the old woman called as we passed through small, cluttered rooms. "Come see who here."

The woman, Lini, could have been Mama, though older, for she had the same eyes, hair, and smile.

"Ma!" Mama cried, shoving us forward and breaking free of our grasp. "George dead. These are the children." As her mother admired us, Mama spoke in the soft voice I heard whenever she spoke with the uncles. "This is your grandmother. Call her Popo Lini," she said, her eyes sweeping the rooms, revealing disappointment. "Where's Da?"

"Da outside in the back garden," Tai Popo replied, padding over to the back door. "Yuping, come inside quick!"

I was almost afraid to breathe in that dim little kitchen with its battered gas range almost as black as the wok that stood atop it. Then I wanted to grasp the very air for support when a giant shadow fell across the floor. But it was no monster. It was my smiling grandfather, and my fears vanished.

Mama hastily told us that before we were born she had cut ties with her parents after deciding to marry Papa. Her parents had felt that Papa was unstable, though she saw marriage to a businessman as an escape from Johns Lane poverty and went ahead with her plan.

Grandfather Yuping had the physique of a much younger

man, though back then he was approaching seventy. He had a ready smile, and how his moustache tickled our faces.

"You are so like your mother," he said, looking intently into our little oval faces. Then he twirled little Katryn above his head while Megan and I watched, fearful that she might bump against the ceiling, but she never did.

When we sold all our household items and moved in with our grandparents, Mama immediately began talking about selling Papa's business and relocating to Caracas. She said business was booming there, but never once mentioned the possibility of our going along with her. We learned later that one of the uncles, Karl Linstrom, a Swede, helped her get established in Latin America. So the business was sold and Mama's plans went smoothly. However, just as she was about to leave the island with Karl, Tai Popo died in her sleep. Everyone said it was due to a broken heart, but Mama did not alter her plans. She and Karl left for Caracas before the funeral, leaving us in grief with Popo Lini and Grandfather Yuping.

Mama barely kept in touch. She said she was not one for writing letters, and phone calls were too expensive. Her few letters were remote and showed no sympathy for the fact that we were frightened children in a house of recent death.

Gradually we befriended some of the children on Johns Lane, very few of whom were Chinese, since it was a predominantly black neighbourhood. Barbara Edwards from next door and I began to collaborate by drawing pictures and making up stories about them on the front veranda to relieve the boredom of the long, hot afternoons. We both dreamed of becoming famous, but neither of us were ever sure just how to go about it.

As the months passed, our lives settled into a regular routine, only to be jolted unexpectedly by the sudden illness of our grandfather. He had been active with his gardening, but one evening complained of flulike symptoms. Grandfather treated himself with homegrown herbs and teas, and at first it seemed to us that he was much improved. But our concern mounted when unexpectedly he took a turn for the worse. He refused to be fussed over and insisted he was not ill enough to require a doctor, and besides, doctors were expensive.

Grandfather died peacefully on a Monday evening after his short illness. Days later, when we called Mama in Caracas, she conveyed her sympathy but managed to convince us she was in a worse position, since her business had failed and Karl Linstrom had left her stranded. She did not return to Jamaica as we thought she would. Popo Lini became our sole support, since Mama never sent money home, claiming the mail system could not be trusted, though Popo Lini, who had not worked since the farm, was already stretching her small savings to keep house and home together.

❦

Time flew by without word from our mother, but one day a letter addressed to Mrs. Lini Lee arrived with foreign stamps. We all swore it must be from Mama and gathered around to hear the contents. But the letter was not from Mama; the postmark was Montreal, Canada. It was from Elaine Wong, Papa's younger sister. It turned out that she had remained in Canada when he had chosen to move to Jamaica. She had become a Canadian citizen and was planning a trip to the island to meet us. Popo Lini folded the letter carefully, stuck it in her pocket, and said, "Let's call your mother and find out if she knows anything about this aunt of yours."

We drew even closer as Popo Lini dialled the long-distance number. It took a while for the phone to be answered, and when it was, it was not Mama. It was a man named Ramirez who said that Fiona Wong was no longer living at that address, as she had, in fact, disappeared after going in search of her companion, a Mr. Linstrom. Popo Lini was devastated, and when I took the receiver from her trembling hands, I found the chatty Ramirez claiming that he himself would have married Mama, had she stayed.

"She never talked of family in Jamaica," he said, assuring us that because of his feelings for her he was doing everything possible to locate her. But in spite of his efforts we never saw our mother again.

"Foolish girl, that Fiona," Popo Lini often grumbled. "Always chasing dreams." And she would turn her head aside so that we would not see her tears.

We were in deep sorrow, unable to attend to many household duties, and clung to one another for even more support. It was sometime before we realized that Aunt Elaine would soon be visiting the island. We grew weary surveying our meagre possessions, the clutter, the sparse furniture, and the stacks of Chinese newspapers Grandfather Yuping had kept, thinking he would find time to read them. The prospect of putting the house in order was overwhelming, and in the end we decided to leave things as they were.

Aunt Elaine arrived smelling of roses and lilacs. She was probably in her early thirties, with a round face like Papa's, though unlike him, she wore a broad smile. She laughed a lot and brought sunshine into the house as she looked deeply into our faces and hugged and kissed us, apologizing for not having contacted us sooner. She was eager to learn our history and told us her parents had briefly returned to China, where they passed away during the time of a fatal fever. Aunt Elaine had stayed behind in Montreal with relatives while completing her studies. Through tears she explained that her brother, our father, was always depressed and had often threatened suicide. She had lost contact with him for more than eighteen years and had only recently found out about us.

"This mustn't happen to us," she said firmly. "I want to be a part of your lives, and my husband feels the same way."

We had not even considered the possibility that she had a husband, and eagerly asked questions about him.

"You'll find out everything you need to know by asking him yourself," she said, laughing. "He's on his way here. He wanted us to have an hour or so together before he joined us."

"He's coming here?" Katryn asked.

"Yes," Aunt Elaine replied, "and he can hardly wait to meet you all."

❦

Sean, Aunt Elaine's husband, was a young man in his late twenties with curly strawberry-blond hair that took us by surprise, since we had given no thought to the fact that he might not be Chinese. I wondered what Popo Lini thought of him, knowing that in some ways she was traditional. But I need not have worried, for when she offered her best homemade herbal teas and sweet cakes in welcome, I knew all was well. Sean assured her that her sweet cakes were the finest he had ever had.

"He sounds like Grandfather Yuping," Popo Lini said with a laugh. "He used to say anything to get a second helping."

Everyone laughed, and for a brief moment I could have sworn Grandfather Yuping was there to share the joke.

What happened next still amazes me and always turns my mind in a somersault. Aunt Elaine, with her hands straining to engulf us all, giggled and said the most astounding thing. "What Uncle Sean and I actually came down to Jamaica for is to arrange to bring you all up to Canada. It's something I had wanted to do but couldn't afford until now. And another thing, Uncle Sean and I own a home large enough for all of us to rattle around in, even Popo Lini."

I could not believe my ears or my good fortune. Canada would be a dream come true. Perhaps I could even become a writer if I studied hard enough, and as for my sisters, they could become anything they wanted. And, best of all, we would not be parted from Popo Lini. But then I had a sinking feeling in my stomach. What if Popo Lini did not want to leave? I turned to face her and shivered. "Can we all go, Popo Lini?" I asked tentatively, afraid of what might come.

Popo Lini smiled, her eyes crinkling at the corners. "There will be no more partings. We will all go. The family must stick together."

An African Out in the Cold

*T*he day in mid-September when Jomo Kalow arrived in Toronto was stifling hot. It was the sort of day when parched leaves clung fearlessly to brittle tree branches in the last vestiges of a blazing summer.

It had taken great courage on Jomo's part to make the journey alone, and at twenty-five years old this was not only his first trip away from his homeland in Africa, but also his first time away from home. All his life he, being the youngest child, had been protected by parents and siblings. His mother especially feared for his safety travelling alone, since of all her grown children, Jomo alone had retained the temperament of a sweet child and she feared that he was somewhat developmentally challenged.

When Jomo's plane landed at Pearson International Airport that evening, the sky was already painted russet. As the plane lost altitude, he could see tall buildings standing like dark sentries against the panoramic sunset that domed the city. He did not know that even as his plane descended the temperature outside had plunged rapidly, causing the city's inhabitants to pull shawls, sweaters, and light jackets reluctantly across their shoulders against the early chill.

Alighting from the plane with other weary passengers, Jomo felt as though he had stepped into a long air-conditioned tunnel, then he recognized the pungent odours of diesel fuel and gasoline in the air.

How could his friend, Anjoli, live in such air? he wondered as he walked the length of the tunnel over the tarmac, replaying in his mind dreams he had had of this very arrival. According to Anjoli's letters, this country was full of wonders. He had read and reread those letters, hardly able to believe he was actually invited to visit such a country. And now he was here, thanks not only to his sheer determination, but also to the assistance of his large family and circle of friends.

When he passed through customs and immigration, the number of people at the airport overwhelmed him, and he knew that finding Anjoli would not be as easy as the many times he had rehearsed this scenario in his mind. Unable to speak English, he was filled with fear and was as lost as a cat in an ocean. He stood stock-still, trying to make sense of his surroundings, only to be bombarded with confusion from all sides. Then his ears pricked up as a familiar sound reached him, and he searched the crowds excitedly. There it was again.

"Jooooomo!" someone called, hurling himself through the wall of people. Then, suddenly, he was face-to-face with Anjoli.

Eight years of separation melted away in that momentous embrace as the two men wept freely on each other's shoulder, oblivious to stares and their damp cheeks. Anjoli, who was five years older than Jomo, seemed to have aged much more rapidly in Canada than Jomo, who had remained at home. Flecks of grey dotted Anjoli's black hair, and his light brown eyes seemed weary. He had spent many tireless hours in preparation for this reunion, working overtime in the factory when other workers had long gone home to hot meals. He had at last found a way to partially repay Jomo the debt he owed him, for Jomo had saved his life many years before when they were still boys. If it were not for Jomo, who had always been considered "slow," Anjoli would have drowned in a rapidly moving river, where he, a non-swimmer, had waded in too far. Without a thought for his own safety, Jomo, a much younger boy, had made the rescue by clinging to overhanging rocks, tree roots, and branches, managing to bring Anjoli safely to shore. What was a trip to Canada, he thought, compared to the gift of life Jomo had given him?

Having lived frugally for years, Anjoli hoped that Jomo would find his meagre possessions and his small apartment pleasing. These thoughts raced through his mind as the two friends huddled against the wind outside the terminal, waiting for a bus to the city. Jomo smiled shyly, slipping his hands into his pockets. "It's cold here, isn't it?" he said.

Anjoli returned his smile. "I brought you a sweater, my friend." Anjoli's whole being ached with the emotion of the reunion, feeling as though a part of home had crossed the ocean to claim him. He wondered how he could possibly tell Jomo his troubles, then decided he wouldn't spoil his friend's visit by telling him about his heart disease.

In spite of his euphoria Jomo was exhausted. He fell asleep on the bus and again on the subway, and had to be jolted awake by Anjoli as they pulled into Sherbourne station.

"This is our stop," Anjoli said. Then the friends walked out into the evening air, each carrying a suitcase.

With shining eyes Jomo marvelled at the buildings, the stores, the lights, the cars, and the people who wandered the street. "Is this your home?" he asked when they arrived at Anjoli's building and the familiar address brought him a rush of pleasure.

"It's not all mine," Anjoli said, laughing as they climbed the broad steps of one of the more modest apartment buildings.

"This looks like a good place to live," Jomo whispered hoarsely.

Anjoli turned his head away, thinking that it was funny that Jomo didn't see the dusty lobby and the worn furniture quite in the same light as he did.

The small apartment was welcoming, and Jomo's eyes brimmed with tears. "I'm here at last" was all he could say as he surveyed the sparsely furnished rooms.

"The TV is on cable," Anjoli said. "We can watch many channels. Tomorrow I'll take you out in the morning, but I have to work in the afternoon." Even before he finished speaking, Anjoli realized Jomo was fast asleep, having curled into a ball on the couch.

By eight o'clock the following morning, they were both up. Anjoli made a pot of tea and buttered thick slices of toast for breakfast. They ate in silence while birds twittered at the third-floor window and sunbeams danced on the walls, far above the roar of traffic in Sherbourne Street below.

"It's going to be a nice day," Anjoli remarked.

When they left the apartment, they found the street clogged with rush-hour traffic. To Jomo, the sidewalks seemed overrun with pedestrians as they walked for what felt like miles and Anjoli pointed out places and landmarks he knew. After an hour or so, Anjoli brought him to a small, bright ice-cream store. It appeared to be a friendly place. The man behind the counter smiled broadly, and when he stood up from his stool, Jomo thought he looked like a big red giant with eyes that were a blue blaze of joy.

"Hello, Anjoli," the giant said. "So this is your friend." He extended his hand to Jomo, who was delighted with the man's firm clasp.

"He's pleased to meet you," Anjoli said, translating for both men, then smiled softly as Jomo bravely spoke the only English phrase he knew.

"The pleasure is mine."

As afternoon approached, the friends headed back to the apartment. Jomo, though exhilarated by the walk, was grateful for a chance to rest. The couch was particularly inviting.

"Well, my friend," Anjoli said, slipping into a light jacket, "I'm off to work, but I've left you an extra key and some money in case you need anything."

Jomo shook his head. "Thanks, but I won't be needing anything."

"Bye then, Jomo, my friend." Anjoli stepped out the door, then called back softly, "Keep the door locked. I'll be home around eleven."

Jomo rose from the couch, waved after Anjoli, then latched the door before once again curling up for a nap. A chill in the air awoke him near midnight. Seeing that the window was still open, he pulled it down securely and looked around for Anjoli, but realized he was alone. He helped himself to a thick slice of bread and unlatched the front door to gaze down the long, dusty corridor, but there was no sign of Anjoli.

Anjoli didn't come home that night, and at daybreak, taking the extra key, Jomo went out in search of him. It was a cold day and the wind had picked up. People huddled at bus shelters, and Jomo wasn't warm enough. He returned to the apartment, half expecting to find Anjoli there, but he was disappointed. He continued his search in the afternoon, shivering noticeably, his light cotton clothes no match for the early fall-like weather. Being shy, and unable to speak the language, he decided not to leave the apartment again.

Days went by, during which he spent his time staring out the window and making pots of tea. When the last of the bread was gone, he ate soda crackers. By the end of the second week, there was little left to eat. From where he sat at the window, he could see people pass by with all manner of food and drink. His stomach heaved with hunger, and he noticed a relentless chill seep in under the windowsill.

Finally, one morning in desperation, he slipped into one of

Anjoli's warm sweaters that he found in the closet and braced himself against the cold. Trudging through the streets, Jomo felt light-headed and frozen as he gazed unseeingly into the eyes of strangers. Then, after what seemed like many blocks from home, he accidentally bumped into someone. His feet gave way beneath him, and in a blur of remembering, the stranger looked oddly familiar. It was the giant from the ice-cream store!

Jomo wondered what the man was saying as he took his arm and steadied him, then led him along the street and sat him down inside the little shop, which wasn't far away. Jomo's cheeks were wet with unexpected tears, for the man produced a hot cup of coffee, which Jomo drank thirstily as he tried to explain his predicament. But the language barrier was too great, and he watched hopefully as his rescuer made a phone call.

Soon a priest walked into the shop, and he and the giant spoke rapidly to each other. The priest was full of concern. "Are you in trouble?" he asked. "Bob here says he knows your friend Anjoli."

Jomo could hardly believe his ears. The priest was speaking in his dialect.

The priest, seeing his surprise, smiled. "I was stationed in Africa near Anjoli's village."

"My...my friend Anjoli has disappeared," Jomo stammered. "And I'm hungry. I haven't eaten in days."

"He needs a hot meal," the priest told Bob in English.

The shopkeeper immediately went to the back of the store, then returned with a steaming bowl of soup and grinned. "He can share my lunch. I don't know how many times Anjoli has shared a meal with me."

While Jomo ate the thick soup, the priest made several phone calls. It was a while before he rejoined Bob and Jomo at the little table.

"I have found your friend," he announced excitedly. "I called various institutions and hospitals."

"Is he all right?" Jomo asked.

"Yes," the priest said. "But he's in the hospital. He had a severe heart attack and required immediate surgery. He was unconscious for some time and has only just come around."

The African wept freely over the hot soup, shivering with joy.

"I'll take you to see him," the priest said.

Jomo smiled for the first time since Anjoli disappeared.

Segovia Stories

*C*arlos Fernandez Segovia has dreams. His dreams flow like the rushing waters of a never-ending waterfall through his fertile mind and become nebulous and arresting tales. It is more than fitting that when I first encountered him he was in the fiction section of the library where I work, surrounded by some of the world's finest literature. I was immediately drawn to him, for although he was an adult, he reminded me of a lost boy with that slight crease in his forehead and his hands stuck stubbornly into his pockets. He was attractively dressed in Italian casual wear, but when he spoke I realized he was Latin American. He asked me for assistance in finding Shakespeare's plays, and at close scrutiny I couldn't help but be arrested by his handsome profile, even as I steered him into the drama section where I felt a secret satisfaction as his broad hands caressed each book lovingly. He must have been twenty-nine or thirty, and his ponytailed hair was as dark as his eyes. I could see an appreciative smile on his sensuous lips as I pointed out each title to him.

The hush in that room must have held enchantment. Perhaps that is why he didn't see me as the boring middle-aged helpful black female librarian that I am, but as a sympathetic ear, for he proceeded to engage me in conversation and spoke passionately about wanting to write plays as potent and tragic as Shakespeare's. He said he was searching out competent actors to play demanding roles in a film he was producing. The leading lady would be black, and coincidentally would be a librarian who had suffered a broken heart. She would spend her days whiling away time in the contemplation of her ideal man. This man, he said, would naturally be Hispanic and full of dreams, as well as passionate about wanting to write a North American screenplay about unrequited love. Ultimately this screenplay would result in the fictional character attending Toronto's annual film festival as a contributing filmmaker. Carlos Fernandez Segovia said the filmmaker should be played by none other than Antonio Banderas, the actor, or a reasonable look-alike. It was by no stretch of the imagination that I observed that Carlos Fernandez Segovia would have been perfect for the part.

From that very first meeting I had the feeling that Carlos Fernandez Segovia accepted me for what I was, warts and all. He invited me out for coffee and beer, none of which materialized since he either couldn't make it at the last minute or else he became too passionate when we got together in his flat and never made it out. But there were quiet times, too, and those are the moments I relish, for his dreams would come spilling out like little fish that cascade over dangerous rocks in a swift river.

"I must tell you about Milagros," he once said. "She's my older cousin. We grew up together in Ecuador. I was five when she was sixteen, and she was the most beautiful, delicate creature I had ever seen. Her hair was as dark as the interior of a forest, and her eyes as blue as the Pacific. And such skin—smooth as glass and radiant! But I, little Carlos, was just a scrawny boy, all knees, tall for my age, nothing exciting to speak of. I still can't understand why Milagros could never take her eyes off me. I would often catch her staring, and her expression reminded me of the way one would stare at a delicious cake. Then one day she took me aside.

"'Do you like kisses?' she asked.

"'No!' I said stubbornly as Milagros held me in an aquamarine gaze.

"'Well, I'll kiss you, anyway.' She kissed me full on the lips and held me fast until I found myself enjoying the feeling of being smothered by her. It felt to me as though my very eyes had gone blurry, and the rest of me had turned to cotton balls.

"'One more little kiss, Milagros,' I pleaded when she pulled away.

"'No, Carlito,' she said sulkily. 'That's enough until you are older.'

"Even though I was so young I couldn't help but realize that Milagros was using me as a sort of target practice, since she was already the love interest of all the best-looking boys in our city. She was totally unmoved by the attention her beauty stirred, and then she attracted handsome José García, the young captain of our local soccer team. At seventeen José was well built and smouldered with sensuality—the perfect match for Milagros.

"One day he asked her out, and in her excitement she spent hours getting ready for the date. She found the perfect dress and the best hairstyle and makeup that made her already perfect eyes sparkle. She was nothing short of a vision. However, when José arrived to pick her up, he was fresh from a soccer game—sweaty, frowzy, and mud-stained. He obviously had no idea how much importance Milagros had placed on the occasion. Therefore, it was I, young Carlos Fernandez Segovia who reprimanded him on his oversight and put him to shame. Since then Milagros has had no use for macho men. In fact, she ended up marrying a cultured stockbroker from London, England, where she now resides as an aristocrat."

Carlos Fernandez Segovia says it was Milagros who first turned him on to kisses, and that she was also the one who made him realize that women of all ages can be beautiful. I, a librarian who loves tales, was so totally fascinated by the story of Milagros that I imagined her as a young Elizabeth Taylor and found myself astonished by the beauty of the Segovia family.

Months later Milagros's story still haunted me. When I saw Carlos Fernandez Segovia again, I asked if he was still in touch with her and if she had ever contacted him. Carlos Fernandez Segovia looked at me blankly like an innocent child. "Who's Milagros?" he asked. And in that significant moment it dawned on me that Carlos Fernandez Segovia's stories are legends. Some he remembers, others he forgets, and they are not all necessarily based on fact.

Once, I invited Carlos Fernandez Segovia to breakfast at my place. We lounged around in chairs, drank tall glasses of orange juice, and ate fried eggs, dumplings, and cod fritters. He told me he enjoyed my cooking, then leaned back in his chair, utterly relaxed.

"This reminds me of the breakfasts we used to have in my country when I was growing up," he said. "Those were the best, and I remember my mother liked to have houseguests. One summer we had visitors from Montreal, a woman who was Mama's old friend from school and her beautiful daughter, Carmela, as well as their boxer dog, Pepito. The *señora* was very prim and proper. I imagine our mothers thought Carmela and I would behave like brother and sister. But we had other ideas. We couldn't take our hands off each other. The moment we were alone, supposedly taking the dog for walks, we would use the opportunity to explore each other fully. I was fourteen and very much in love, although Carmela was almost eighteen. But summers don't last forever and Carmela would soon return to Canada. She told me her mother was so religious and proper that she would never accept our relationship, so we should keep everything undercover, so to speak.

"One hot afternoon Carmela and I were so eager for each other that halfway from home we realized we had forgotten to bring the dog. Reluctantly we returned to the little guest cottage behind my house and were about to call Pepito when I noticed a strange silence in the compound. No one was home in the big house where I lived, so I thought perhaps that Mama had gone shopping. But suddenly our ears were filled with the sounds of groans. Carmela and I approached the guest cottage with caution and, peering through a half-drawn curtain, we saw Carmela's mother and Pepito in a compromising position. You can well imagine how startled she was to see us. After that Carmela and I lost the attraction for each other, and I suppose she still lives in Montreal and that she and her mother have both forgotten me."

Carlos Fernandez Segovia told me he has another cousin, also called Carlos, who was starting a clothing firm in Canada and that they would be travelling together to Montreal to make contacts and perhaps rent a factory. When he left a few days later, it occurred to me that now that he was an adult, he might well resume his relationship with Carmela. On his return to Toronto he telephoned to say he had indeed seen Carmela. She was more beautiful than ever, but unfortunately was married to a wonderful French Canadian and had four young children and a happy but boring life. I wondered if Carlos Fernandez Segovia and Carmela had taken the family dog for a walk or, if like Milagros, Carmela had ever existed.

The next time I heard from Carlos Fernandez Segovia he telephoned to say he was helping out a friend who had overdosed on drugs and was hospitalized. He wanted tea and sympathy, and I was happy to oblige. Carlos Fernandez Segovia proceeded to show me photographs of actors he had chosen for his film. "Filming begins in March," he said. Sure enough, the leading actress was black. I felt a prick of jealousy, for the actress was beautiful. Carlos Fernandez Segovia must have sensed my emotion, because he said, "Surely you didn't think you were my first Jamaican. My father is a physician in Ecuador and we used to entertain diplomats. I couldn't take my hands off the daughter of the Jamaican ambassador. I can't remember if her name was Carmela. It was so long ago."

Carlos Fernandez Segovia often spoke of his immediate family: his father, who is now a cancer specialist; his European drop-dead gorgeous blond mother; and his two brothers, Simón and Hernán. Photographs on the walls of his flat are proof of their existence. They are placed directly beside the photographs of the actors, but it is interesting to note that filming on his picture has still not begun.

"My brother, Hernán, is not like me," Carlos Fernandez Segovia said, pointing at the photograph. He is quite blond, as you can see." I noted that his brother looked suspiciously like Brad Pitt. "He is very handsome and wants to be a graphic artist. And although he is only twenty-one, he once had a fiancée. The girl's name is Bianca. Hernán studies day and night, but he makes short films and videos as a hobby. He has a little studio in our home. His equipment is very expensive, so he set up a surveillance camera in the studio without telling anyone, not even Bianca. She used to sneak into our home when he was away and wait in his studio for his return. But she began to feel neglected and wrote Hernán a threatening note, saying she would kill herself if she couldn't see more of him. Needless to say, Hernán was upset, especially when she continued to make it clear she didn't want to live without him and constantly spoke of suicide. Our family was surprised when Hernán gave her her walking papers. We couldn't believe he was so cold, for Bianca was so devoted. But Hernán later revealed that on replaying his surveillance tapes he had caught Bianca on film in the arms of our gardener on all the occasions when she was supposedly waiting for him."

Carlos Fernandez Segovia told me that one of his best friends back home in Ecuador was an older man of about sixty-eight who had been a real ladykiller in his youth. This man had recently died of AIDS, which caused Carlos Fernandez Segovia to speak somewhat regretfully about an occasion when he and friends had visited a gay bar in Toronto and he was kissed on the lips by one of the male dancers. I reassured him that AIDS wasn't spread by kisses, and he confided that that kiss was the best he had ever had. What of Milagros? I wondered.

It was only on rare occasions that friends of mine even met Carlos Fernandez Segovia, for he was almost always unavailable. However, I did get him to meet my publisher friend, Martha Cox, at a dinner at my place. He regaled her with stories of his trip to the gay bar and told her a tale about a young friend, Harry Perron, who he had met at acting class. According to him, Harry was set up by a woman in the Dominican Republic who claimed he was the father of her unborn child. She tried to bilk him out of thousands of dollars, being totally unaware that Harry was gay. Carlos Fernandez Segovia said that Harry told fabulous stories and was the one who had recently told him about a Canadian man who several years ago went skiing in the B.C. interior, got lost during an avalanche, and was presumed dead. Years later this same man's son, Ethan, went skiing in the same region and, by coincidence, was also caught in an avalanche. While lost he came upon a wall of ice, and in it he encountered a face staring at him. The visage mirrored his own, and he realized that it was his father's face trapped in ice for all those years. He and his father, in that precise moment, looked about the same age. The young man collapsed from shock but was later rescued. Although he searched, he never again could find the face in the wall of ice.

"I should write a screenplay about it," Carlos Fernandez Segovia said. "It would have such plot, such drama and suspense, even more than anything by Shakespeare. I must ask Harry for all the details."

Martha Cox said that Carlos Fernandez Segovia was a little too slick for her, but with his looks she could forgive him anything. The only thing, though, she said, was that his stories were far too realistic. No one would buy them.

"I want to write a screenplay about a family from your country," Carlos Fernandez Segovia told me excitedly once. "Perhaps you could help me with naming people and locations. I would also like to write about a poor man from Peru who wins the lottery, and I'll let him also write a screenplay about a young filmmaker who goes to Hungary to a film festival. These two stories are very tempting. Maybe I'll call one of the Jamaicans, Sheila, since that is your name, and I'll let her meet a young Hispanic man called Julio. I love the plot but don't know what to do with Julio. Should I kill him? That would make an interesting plot. Maybe he could be a bad man, or perhaps a man like me. Help me. I value your advice."

The last time I saw Carlos Fernandez Segovia we were in a bar on College Street, the trendy part, and he told me he was late arriving because a friend of his, an older man of sixty-eight, had been drinking in a sixth-floor apartment and had accidentally toppled over the balcony. I wondered if this was the same older man who had previously died in Ecuador from AIDS.

I never did help Carlos Fernandez Segovia with his stories, because the next time I went to visit him he wasn't home. His neighbours told me he had been admitted to a mental institution in Toronto. They said he was either not allowed visitors or he himself had requested not to see anyone. Yet, though unable to visit him, I often imagine him in the institution surrounded by other patients and even doctors, that strange otherness about him as he takes centre stage and mesmerizes them with tales as he once did me. For surely Carlos Fernandez Segovia's dreams still flow like a never-ending waterfall.

Villa Fair

The House

*T*here was no other stone house as large as Villa Fair for miles around. It was originally built in the seventeenth century by a British landowner who had come to live on August Island in the Caribbean Sea, and it was he who chose its unique hilltop location.

The interior of the house was spacious. Five sun-drenched bedrooms and a bathroom stood on either side of a wide hall that ran the entire length of the second floor. A broad, winding oak staircase connected the floors. On the main floor there was an airy dining room, a living room, a study, and an oak-panelled library with exquisite views of purple mountain ridges on one side and glimpses of the distant aquamarine sea on the other. The front parlour had a passageway that led directly to the kitchen and the pantry, and immediately behind were the servants' quarters, which in the old days had housed slaves.

A wide veranda ran on three sides of the house, and the bay windows on the main floor had the advantage of looking out over a magnificent rose garden, so perfectly tended that August Island's wilderness had not reclaimed it. Behind the house were stables, large enough for eight horses.

Broad stone steps at the entrance of the house led down to a gravel path that widened into a meandering dirt road that came to a sudden stop where wilderness finally intruded and cultivated crops of coconuts, bananas, and sugarcane began.

Many ghosts must have walked the halls of Villa Fair, because many of its inhabitants had passed away over the years.

Geraldine

When Geraldine Belmont first came to August Island, she was a young woman of twenty, but these days everyone called her Granny. She was old now and felt a certain kinship with the house as she sat in the sunshine on the veranda, wagging her silver head, trying to remember all that had happened through the years, recalling how the blatant beauty of August Island enthralled her then and still did. She was well into her eighties now but had been born in England. The house was far older than she was, though it had been in the Belmont family for many years. It belonged to the family of her husband, William, whom she had come to join on the island. It was a daring adventure on her part, a risk she felt well worth taking, for she loved William from the first time she saw him.

William Belmont's parents were English, though he was born on August Island and had grown up closer to the ways of the dark-skinned locals than those of his British heritage. At twenty-four he had decided to settle into farming the plantation where Villa Fair's house stood, but on his father's insistence he travelled to England to study accounting. His father saw the wisdom of William becoming proficient in financial and economical matters.

But not only did William find it difficult to adapt to life in England and the incessant cold, he also found it hard to excel in his studies. It was Howard Chambers, a middle-aged professor who ran the boarding house where William lodged in Yorkshire, who took pity on the young man, placed him under his wing, and gave him private lessons. The professor, seeing that William could also use some culture to soften his rough rural edges, introduced him to opera, ballet, and theatre. In spite of it, blond-haired William's manner of speech and attitude remained that of a country-born islander. Howard would often shake his head and mutter, "This is what colonization does to our people."

Howard's son, Ian, was five years older than William, and every inch an English gentleman. William might have learned some of his ways, since he was a younger man, but unfortunately Ian no longer lived at home, having taken up residence in Brighton. Howard was never sure what it was that attracted his teenage daughter, Geraldine, to William. He himself had known what it was to be in love, for he had loved Ian and Geraldine's mother, Alice, up until her death ten years earlier.

Geraldine adored her father and thought nothing of confiding her feelings to him. Howard laughed good-naturedly, accusing his daughter of trying to make a silk purse out of William.

Geraldine still remembers when she first spoke to William. She had been crossing a wide, overgrown field near the boarding house, the wild wind pasting her heavy skirts to her slim frame and playing havoc with her broad hat.

"William!" she called out, seeing him up ahead, looking like a lost lamb. He wasn't wearing a topcoat, though it was mid-November, and when she saw his hands, they were white with cold. "You'll catch your death!" she shouted.

William only chuckled, his blue eyes ablaze in drizzly Yorkshire. "It reminds me a little of home. These fields make me homesick."

"Where's home?" she asked, already knowing full well where he was from, since her father often mentioned it.

"August Island," he replied, a slight smile warm on his lips. "My parents are English."

Before he turned his head away, Geraldine thought she noticed a tear in his eye.

He sighed. "I miss the island so much. I'd do anything to be going home."

"Do you mind if I walk with you?" she asked, hoping to prolong the brief conversation.

"I don't mind. It's getting quite chilly now."

William

*W*illiam and Geraldine entered the boarding house through a side door and were in time to meet with Howard Chambers, who had been on his way upstairs to his study. Howard paused on the stairs, noticing the curious excitement in his daughter's eye and William's look of nostalgia.

"William," he said, "there's a telegram for you in the hall. I almost forgot. I hope it's not bad news."

William turned away, thoughts racing, as Howard continued up the stairs. Geraldine, who couldn't bear to desert William, followed him at a distance. By the time she entered the hall, William was sitting at the carved hall table that had been her mother's. William's head was in his hands, and the telegram spread out before him.

Hearing her footsteps, he looked up briefly, his face as pale as the white roses in the vase next to him. "I'm going home," he said shakily.

"What's happened?" Geraldine asked.

"My father has passed away. They buried him yesterday. It would have been too long for them to wait for my return, but now I must go home."

Geraldine bent and touched his hand lightly, then placed her pale cheek against his. She wanted to hold him, keep him safe, but instead she whispered in his ear, "I'm so very sorry. I wish you didn't have to go."

William's cold hands barely felt the warmth of hers. Of course, he was attracted to her, but the heavy burden of suddenly having to run a plantation had already begun to weigh him down. What would become of his mother? he wondered. Since her marriage, she had never been separated from her husband, and his poor father had never really thought about death.

"I'll be leaving the day after tomorrow," he finally said hoarsely. "I'll need to make arrangements."

"I want to come with you," Geraldine said. "Marry me, William! Take me home as your wife."

William did not return home in two days as he had thought. He married Geraldine in a small stone church on a cold, damp morning. Howard Chambers and his son, Ian, were the only persons in attendance besides the two strangers who served as witnesses, because Geraldine felt that if William's family and friends could not be there, the wedding should be spare, especially so soon after the death of his father.

Almost immediately after the wedding, William returned to August Island alone. On his arrival he found that his mother had been desperate for his return. She was bedridden and fragile with grief, and William could see that her eyes were hollow with waiting for death.

"I'll not be long for this world," she whispered, clutching him close. "You'll need a wife to be mistress of the plantation."

"I was married in England," William confessed. "Her name is Geraldine. She is English."

"You must send for her then," his mother pleaded, a small flicker of pleasure on her wan face.

William kissed her cool cheek and promised he would, and

when his mother died that night, a terrible calm settled about the house. But there was no peace there, for it was a house of sorrow.

William did not send for Geraldine immediately. Instead, in grief, he set about making repairs to the house. So, with one thing or another, particularly running the plantation, time slipped by and he lost sight of his duty. A whole year had passed when Geraldine sent word that she would be arriving by ship, and William was jolted into reality.

The reunion was a passionate one, and Geraldine felt that William must have been starved for affection, because he ravished her with bitter kisses and tore at her fine clothes. She was delighted with his lovemaking, which took place both inside the house and outside in the wild. It often crossed her mind that a man with such passion in his loins as William had could not have remained faithful to her in that year of separation. But she let her suspicions melt away under the heat of his lovemaking; she did not even mind when she became pregnant.

Thunder

*T*he baby was born at Villa Fair on an afternoon of pelting rain—not the soft rains of spring but rain that came with the violence of a fierce storm. Strong winds uprooted trees and scattered timber like toothpicks. Lightning forked the sky, and the storm's ferocity prevented Geraldine's doctor from attending. Instead, the baby was delivered by two black servant women, Miriam and Sheba, who together guided an exhausted Geraldine through the birth. By twilight a sturdy baby boy was delivered into the hands of his father, for William hovered feverishly over the proceedings, afraid of the outcome.

Geraldine called the baby Thunder because his thick, ruby-tinged hair was as dark as the storm outside; and when she saw his pale eyes, they reminded her of the white lightning that lit up the skies. She also felt that Thunder would be a suitable name for such a strong-looking child.

❦

Thunder Belmont *was* strong. He ruled the household from the first moment of his birth. His every small cry brought the cool, dark, comforting hands of Miriam and Sheba; the warm cooing of his mother; the incessant curiosity of his father. William adored the child, and when he held him to his breast and felt the baby's small heart beating, tears welled in his eyes.

By the time Thunder was eight, he had been to England twice. And he, like his father before him, yearned to return to the island's warmth, the plantation, and its people.

As Thunder grew older, he became tall and strong, towering over William. He was a quick learner and devoured education like a hungry piranha. He spent most of his hours in study, his dark hair falling languidly across his eyes as he became lost in concentration. At school his classmates, who were mostly blacks, accepted him as one of their own, and the dark-haired girls with their braids would giggle among themselves, claiming he was impossibly handsome.

Thunder was the fourth grandchild of Howard Chambers. Ian, Geraldine's brother, had long ago married in Brighton and was a widower. He was left with three children: Elizabeth, nineteen; Seth, eighteen; and Cameron, sixteen, the same age as Thunder.

It was in his sixteenth year that Thunder again went to England. He and his cousins gathered in their grandfather's house, which excited Howard Chambers, who believed the presence of young people rejuvenated him. He was particularly fond of Thunder and listened with pride when the youngster, around a roaring fire, talked passionately about his life on August Island.

Thunder spoke eloquently about the island's black population and of the few British families he knew there. He spoke of wooden shacks that leaned into the wind, the estate mansions, the bustling capital city, and the vast plantations. He spoke of the cries of the colourful tropical birds, and of fishermen coming home at dusk to beaches bathed in gold and silver sunlight. He even spoke of the great black vultures that flew across the sky, and how the common folk cooked wonderful meals on open fires in the fields. Then he would speak of the wild vegetation and the crops and try to describe how the sugarcane swayed in the warm breezes like waves upon the sea. Last of all, he would tell the story of Man Man Jefferson, a black ghost boy who supposedly haunted Villa Fair. Then he would yearn for the sounds of the tropics, only to be silenced by the howling wind outside.

The summer he turned seventeen Thunder's cousins came to the island to see it for themselves. The days were filled with long horseback rides; swims in cool ponds and the warm sea; trips to Rozelle, the capital city; and long, lazy evenings on the veranda. And Miriam and Sheba were always on hand with chilled drinks of mint and lime.

Cameron struck up friendships wherever he went, being most like Thunder in temperament. He rode into the wild and spoke with donkey-cart men and labourers working in the hot sun, and he would wave his hat jauntily at the ragged, barefoot black children who walked the narrow paths in the fields, bringing hot lunches to their labourer fathers.

One hot afternoon the whole family, except for Seth, was gathered on the broad veranda playing cards. William saw the sky redden and noticed how silent the once-raucous birds had become.

"We're to have a storm," he said, anxiously eyeing the horizon.

"Will Seth be all right?" Geraldine wondered out loud, knowing her nephew had gone horseback riding on his own.

"He knows the way well," Thunder said. "He only went as far as Lionel's Crossing."

"That's not too far," Geraldine said, settling back into the game. But as she spoke, the sky darkened menacingly and a deep silence hung over the plantation. "We'd best be getting inside."

Without warning the sky split like a torn black curtain and a great white gash ripped through the clouds. Rain drenched the sloping green lawn, and a terrible rumble shook the house, alarming them all. The rosebushes in the garden were like tangled thorns, and from a distance the family heard the urgent cries of the servants and field hands desperate for shelter.

"Inside everyone!" William said sharply. "The lightning can be dangerous!"

They all moved toward the wide French doors, but only Elizabeth held back. "Look!" she shouted. "Someone's coming."

Andrew

*T*hunder strained his eyes to penetrate the dark sheets of rain as he clutched the veranda rail in anticipation. "It's a horseman. It might be Seth."

When the rider drew close to the house, they all knew it was not Seth. The rider, who was wearing a dark hooded cloak, quickly dismounted and raced up the steps. "Mr. Belmont, come quick! Bring some rope! Your nephew's in the river!"

Elizabeth reeled. "Seth isn't a good swimmer!" She met the rider's cool brown eyes and saw that he was a young man of perhaps her own age. But unlike her, he was black. And when the hood fell around his shoulders, she observed that he had short rain-soaked black curls and that his skin was as dark as mahogany.

"How did it happen?" she asked as William hurried inside to get some rope.

"I think his horse threw him," the boy said calmly. "I didn't see it myself, but I was out rounding up my father's animals when I heard the thunder. It frightened the animals, and then I heard shouts. I went to investigate and looked over the side of a steep ravine. I saw a boy struggling to keep his grip on a tree that had been hit by lightning and was floating in the river. He was holding on to the roots, but I wasn't able to reach him. I shouted to him that I'd get help because I needed a rope. Then, when last I looked, the current had begun to pull the tree out into rough water. The horse is still at the top of the ravine, waiting."

The boy was well spoken, and it was Elizabeth's guess that he was both educated and intelligent.

"What's your name, son?" William said, returning with a huge coil of rope.

"It's Andrew Innsford. My father owns the next plantation."

"Thank you, Andrew," William said. "Let's go."

Then he strode across the yard to the stables, unmindful of the pelting rain. Thunder and Cameron followed close behind, and Elizabeth raced after them.

"Be careful," Geraldine called out as the five riders galloped past, led by Andrew.

When the riders approached the ravine, Drummer Boy, Seth's horse, was still at the top of the incline. As soon as the horse saw the riders, he shuddered. William quickly dismounted. "Boys, tie this end of the rope to Drummer Boy. I'll climb down with the other end."

"No, Father!" Thunder cried. "I'll climb down. I know all these rivers and ravines, and I'm the best swimmer."

Andrew, too, slipped from his horse. "I'll come with you."

There was no time for argument. After tying the rope around Drummer Boy, the two boys lowered themselves into the ravine. Its walls were slippery with rain, and the riverbank was swollen with the torrent.

"Will they be all right, Uncle William?" Cameron asked.

"Thunder's a very strong boy," William replied absently. Then the rope slackened, and William shouted to the boys below, "Are you all right? Have you seen him?"

But only the sound of the pounding rain came to his ears, and a sudden chill crept into his heart and alarmed him, for from where he was he knew the storm had darkened the ravine.

"I see him!" Thunder's voice rang out above the rain. "I see him! He's exhausted, I think, but he's still clinging to the tree root. Luckily it's been stopped midstream. It looks as if it's jammed against a boulder. I'll have to swim out to him."

Thunder did not want to alarm his father, and had not told him of the great distance downriver that Seth and the tree had travelled. He threw off his shirt and dived into the swirling water. The river immediately wrestled with him, tearing at his arms and legs as the rain drove against him. The current pulled him along and threatened to carry him away, but Thunder's brute strength was its equal and he finally pulled alongside Seth.

"Seth, it's Thunder! Put your arms around me. I know you're tired, but it's the only way. Don't let go, and for God's sake, keep your head above the water. I'll get you out of here."

Seth's eyes met his briefly. "I won't let go."

With the added weight of Seth, Thunder began swimming against the current. It was the most difficult swim of his life. At times Seth seemed to pull him under; at other moments his arms and legs felt useless. Determined not to let the river defeat him, he struggled toward shore.

Andrew saw his difficulty and immediately swam out to meet them. "Here, let me help," he said, pulling abreast. Together he and Thunder brought Seth ashore.

When they arrived at the Villa Fair house, Geraldine was pacing the floor of the veranda. Some labourers and servants were keeping her company, and they all ran to meet the weary riders.

"Our son's a hero," William said. "He's the only one of us who could have made that swim to save Seth, but we mustn't forget this other hero in our company—Andrew Innsford."

"Thank God you're all safe," Geraldine sighed, embracing the exhausted William and brashly kissing him full on the lips in front of everyone.

The hired help cheered spontaneously, and when Geraldine spoke to Seth, she was delighted to learn he had suffered nothing more than very sore hands and a sprained ankle.

"It wasn't Drummer Boy's fault," Seth said. "He was spooked by the lightning."

"Please come inside, everyone," Geraldine said, feeling light-headed. "Supper's ready. You, too, Andrew. Come join us. It's the least we can do."

When dinner was over, William asked Andrew, "What do you plan to make of your life?" They were all in the sitting room, and the hired help had returned to their quarters also to feast in celebration of Seth's safe return.

"I want to be a lawyer," Andrew said, a certain shyness creeping into his half smile.

❦

It was with assistance from Geraldine and her father in England that Andrew Innsford was able to attend one of the finest schools in Yorkshire, England, in preparation for law school. Howard Chambers insisted that the young man stay free of charge in his boarding house. But he might have been more astute than he was given credit, for he, though aging, had not missed the spark of passion that had sprung up between Elizabeth and Andrew. He was not sure what to make of it, but felt that with the young man under his roof, he was better able to keep his eye on things, because Elizabeth's father, Ian, certainly would not have approved of a relationship.

Guadeloupe

*U*nlike Andrew, Thunder Belmont did not go to England to study. He remained on August Island. Surprisingly he, too, chose law as a career, and his parents sent him to study in San Carlos, a medium-size town on the other side of the island. Thunder was to study under one of England's finest lawyers who had come to reside on the island. Milton Langley was a household name on both sides of the Atlantic.

San Carlos was where the rich and near-rich British expatriates resided and set up practices. There were many lawyers and doctors there with exquisite and expensive homes, and there was a noticeable absence of locals in the population. San Carlos was also where foreigners descended in search of white sand beaches and balmy breezes. The few locals that did show themselves in the town were mostly vendors.

Thunder lived downtown, renting a few rooms above Langley's office. He was an excellent student, and his days were consumed with study. One late morning he was sitting on the balcony connected to his room. He liked studying there; it overlooked the busy street, and with a few strategically planted shrubs and vines, he maintained a semblance of privacy. His reverie, though, was suddenly disrupted by a woman's angry voice.

"Let me in!" she shouted. "Mr. Langley knows I'm coming! I said let me in!"

Thunder leaned over the balcony to see who was causing the commotion. He spotted a black woman of about thirty-eight standing her ground at the office door below. She was dressed in a cheap low-cut dress designed to show off her figure.

Maggie, the office maid, had tried to prevent the woman from entering, and the disturbance had ensued. A few pedlars and townspeople going about their business had stopped to observe.

Not wanting any embarrassment to the firm, Thunder called down urgently to the woman. "Can I help you?"

The woman stood haughtily, arms akimbo, her heavy mane of rough black hair pulled back from her face. She was not wearing a hat, which was the custom, but her dark eyes blazed like coals and her sensual lips were outlined in red.

"Who you?" the woman demanded, staring up at Thunder and eyeing him in much the same manner one would scrutinize a young colt.

"I'm Thunder Belmont," he replied hastily, forgetting to alter his acquired British accent.

Hearing this, the woman threw back her head and laughed mockingly. "You must be the white boy I hear about that talk like one of us. Why you putting on airs, boy?" She smiled knowingly, revealing perfect white teeth.

Thunder grinned back. He considered her quite daring and felt an immediate attraction to her.

"Can I come in?" she said, tossing her head so that her long, heavy hair cascaded onto her shoulders.

"Let her in," Thunder said, and Maggie immediately did so. As for the small crowd that had gathered, it lost interest and dispersed.

Thunder bounded down the stairs, strangely exhilarated. The woman was already seated in the waiting room. Her legs were held wide apart below her long skirts, and in spite of the heat, she wore short-buttoned boots. Thunder thought she looked like a warrior, and let his mind engage in fantasy. The pout of her lips and the swell of her bosom brought a thin sweat to his brow.

"I'm Guadeloupe MacDaniels," the woman announced without rising, catching him off guard as he stared at her. "Mr. Langley ask me to come here to pick up my divorce papers, and that woman at the door, she try to stop me coming in. She say he not here today, but I know my papers ready."

Thunder was not certain if he was authorized to give her any papers, but the lilt and smokiness of her voice excited him. He went into Langley's adjoining office and bent over the desk, but found it impossible to concentrate. The woman's musky perfume consumed him.

Maggie, who had not left her position as guard, stepped forward. "I have never seen this woman here before," she said to Thunder. "And I doubt Mr. Langley would be doing any kind of business with her."

Guadeloupe immediately rose from her chair, eyes blazing. "Look, Mr. Langley handled my case from him home. Everybody but an idiot knows that him do some business on the side. Him a good man and him know how to stay on top of things."

The insinuation in her words filled Thunder's loins with fire. He again leaned over the desk and, amid the clutter, saw a large brown envelope addressed to Guadeloupe MacDaniels.

Thunder returned to the waiting room in triumph but found Guadeloupe preoccupied with studying his biceps, his slim waist, his light-coloured eyes and the dark lock that hung so carelessly over them.

"This must be what you're after," he said, handing her the envelope, hardly daring to meet her eyes.

Guadeloupe rose and brushed her dark hand against his as she accepted the envelope. Thunder felt her hot breath on his cheek.

"I'm after a lot more than this," she said provocatively. Then she whispered, "Thanks."

That afternoon Thunder went out into the streets, knowing that in Langley's absence he could come and go as he pleased. Vendors were selling trinkets, meaningless little pieces of carved jewellery and shells. The air was pungent with the scent of the sea and the delicious odour of hot meals cooking in large tin vats over coal fires along the streets.

Thunder wandered aimlessly, noticing as though for the first time the many women of San Carlos. Well-dressed white ladies in bonnets nodded at him approvingly with discreet smiles, and young black vendor girls called him "Sir" as they held out their wares for him to see.

His thoughts momentarily turned to Villa Fair. He planned to go home on the weekend after a month's absence and was so caught up with thoughts of home that it startled him when a husky voice spoke next to his ear.

"Looking for me, are you?" Gaudeloupe fell into step with him, a satisfied smile on her lips. "Want a drink?" she asked, mischief in her eyes.

"I don't drink," Thunder replied, inhaling her heavy perfume.

She laughed. "Who says I was offering a little bird like you alcohol?"

Thunder, detecting mockery, felt a need to redeem himself. "I never drink when I'm studying. And I'm not a little bird as you might think. I'm twenty-two."

Guadeloupe hissed loudly and steered Thunder over to a coconut vendor. "I meant coconut water," she said with a wink.

Between sips of coconut water, Thunder told her about Villa Fair and how much he was looking forward to going home.

"You lucky you have such a place to go to," she said gravely. "I live over in Torrence. Ever been there?"

Thunder shook his head. He had heard of the shantytown that bordered San Carlos. It was said to be infested by rats and inhabited by the commonest of blacks, but he kept that knowledge to himself.

"Come there tomorrow on your lunch. There's a lot of things I could show you. My house is the aquamarine one. You can't miss it."

Langley was back at work the next day, and when Thunder mentioned that Guadeloupe MacDaniels had been in to pick up her papers, the man smiled wryly. "She's a strong one. And she always gets what she wants. It has to be her looks."

Thunder did not quite know what to make of Langley's words but found himself crossing into Torrence at lunchtime. Dirty black children in rags hounded him the moment he set foot there. Some begged for coins, others called him "Mr. High Horse" and whined loudly as he went by. A group of eight tired black men sat around on crates playing cards. The cards looked as filthy as their leathery fingers. Stray dogs and pigs rummaged side by side in mounds of garbage, and Thunder began to regret his impulse. But then an old black woman whom he had asked for directions pointed out the aquamarine shanty where Guadeloupe lived.

A half-dozen black children were playing outside with an old rusted iron cartwheel. They ran this way, then that. Guadeloupe stepped boldly between them to meet him.

"Those two are my younger sons," she said, pointing at two of the ragged boys. "My older one is with him father."

Thunder was stunned. He had not expected her to have a family. He followed Guadeloupe nervously up the one step that led into the house, then gave her a small spray of zinnias and ferns. Pleasure danced in her eyes as she quickly filled a dusty jar with water.

"You lucky we have rainwater from the barrel," she said, leaning close and stopping Thunder's heart as she smiled. "Sometimes I be forgetting you so young. I seen a lot. I be forty myself."

She bent low, almost in a squat, to place the jar on an old sea chest. As she did, her loose blouse billowed open like a sail, revealing firm breasts.

Thunder froze, but Guadeloupe only laughed deliciously as though his seeing her like that was the most natural thing in the world.

"Mr. Belmont," she said, straightening, "wouldn't you rather taste my lips?"

Thunder was well aware of the double meaning of her words, and he shuddered. Seizing the moment, Guadeloupe drew closer. Without hesitating, Thunder took her fiercely in his arms, pressed her against him, and kissed her hard. The kiss was nothing like he had expected, because he had not anticipated the intense pleasure or that he would feel as though he were falling into a dark, delicious pit with no chance of escape. He offered no resistance when Guadeloupe expertly guided him into her small, dishevelled bedroom.

Thunder did not go home that weekend or the one after that, and he gave no thought to the possibility that his spending time with Guadeloupe would generate rumours and insinuations. He ignored the fact that a white lawyer boy involved with a middle-aged black woman from the shanties was enough to forge the chains of gossip for a full year. He also forgot that in small districts rumours have wings.

Geraldine and William assumed his absences were due to his heavy study load, so they asked no questions. But finally rumours reached even their ears. A handcart man who had been in San Carlos came to Villa Fair to sell housewares, and he shared what little information he had with the servants, saying that a white boy who looked like Thunder was keeping company with a black harlot in Torrence.

William dismissed the story when he heard it, feeling that if the boy was Thunder it was only a matter of time before the young man came of age and to his senses. Geraldine, however, was disturbed by the information, and though she made careful inquiries, seemed always to come up with nothing, for no one in her circle would name names or establish contacts.

Thunder grew accustomed to the surroundings at Torrence, becoming a permanent fixture in Guadeloupe's shack and giving up his residence above Langley's office. He knew that bringing Guadeloupe there would create a scandal.

One rainy morning in May, Howard Chambers died peacefully in England after a brief illness. On hearing of his grandfather's death, Thunder returned to Villa Fair to be with his mother. No one mentioned the rumours, considering them inappropriate, and there was no reference made to his long absences.

A year after the affair began Guadeloupe gave birth to Thunder's fair-skinned son. It was difficult to imagine the midnight-dark Guadeloupe as the child's mother. The baby shared his father's pale lightning eyes, though his tuft of soft reddish curls was not unlike Geraldine's. They called him Edmund, a strong name.

One evening after supper Guadeloupe remarked that though it was still early, the moon was full. She saw this as a sign to bless the baby's future with moonbeams. She sent her two older sons out to play, then placed the baby in a wicker basket, took it outside, and left it near the shack where the sleeping child would get the best exposure to the moonlight and, ultimately, all the blessings for his future. She claimed the ritual was a traditional practice handed down from her people, but it might have been an excuse to indulge in an early bout of lovemaking without interruption.

Guadeloupe led Thunder back into the shack where their passion ignited. After a while Guadeloupe thought she heard the baby cry out sharply. She became alarmed, and in her haste accidentally knocked over the kerosene lamp she had placed beside the bed. It was the very lamp she used to cast grotesque shadows on the wall to reflect their sexual movements and enhance their passion.

Kerosene spilled onto the floor, and flames quickly shot up. Because there was no privacy in the house, Thunder had culti- vated a habit of dragging a heavy, decrepit wardrobe across the bedroom's low doorway to prevent their being disturbed. That meant there was no window to escape from, and the room quickly filled with smoke as the fire raged, angrily licking the bedclothes, the sea chest, the cradle, and bundles of discarded clothes.

Thunder's eyes were blinded in the intense heat and thick smoke. He became disoriented, unable to find the wardrobe, and his ears were filled with Guadeloupe's screams. He groped frantically as flames leaped up his clothes and sizzled in his hair. Guadeloupe fell against him, scratching and grasping desperately. But Thunder knew there was no escape and that Villa Fair was now forever lost to him.

Driving Through Red Lights

*A*t twenty-three I am already past my prime and should have been married. Those are words I have heard repeatedly from my Bombay-born parents, who won't be convinced otherwise, not even now that they live in Toronto, and not even since I am Canadian-born. I don't know how often I have looked into my mother's eyes and seen disappointment, seen the knowing glance my parents exchange each time my birthday arrives.

My mother prepared me since grade school to be an ideal wife. I remember the many hours we spent in the kitchen when I was barely seven. She expressed pride when my little hands instinctively weighed and measured the appropriate garam masala spices, for my nostrils knew well the pungent odours of ground cardamom, cinnamon, cloves, cumin, coriander, and black pepper. As a result of her diligence, I missed out on the childhood games of Red Rover, Dead Man's Chase, and Simon

Says, being confined to the house, where my prisoner's heart would soar in imagination to join the happy cries of other children outside, while my hands, with a memory all their own, worked alongside my mother's.

"Pay attention," she would say. "Combine flour, lemon juice, chili, and potatoes with spinach and cauliflower and water. Blend it well, then drop a spoonful at a time into hot oil. When it turns golden brown, remove it from the pan and drain on paper towels."

I faithfully followed her instructions, but in adulthood, and with talk of arranging a marriage for me, I feel it is time to find my own way. I don't want an arranged marriage, but I know my protests will fall on deaf ears, because my traditional parents would like nothing better than to improve their status by being the in-laws to a professional man. There seems to be no stopping an avalanche of events that are unfolding, especially since my father has announced that his older sister, my Aunt Rashna, is coming to visit from Bombay.

When Aunt Rashna comes, I am hardly prepared for her sarcasm and interference. Because I have been trained in culinary arts and housework, I think that alone will please her domineering, old-fashioned spirit, but I am wrong. The day after her arrival I help unpack her luggage, hanging her clothes in careful rows, then set about preparing a four-course meal in her honour. Aunt Rashna, without so much as a comment, seems filled with thoughts of her own that, like steam in a gasket, are dying to escape. She sails into our living room, her silken sari sighing against her ample frame.

"I have found someone," she announces enthusiastically.

Momentarily I forget about myself, thinking my aging widowed aunt is primed for marriage again.

"I have found someone for Kamla," she adds, startling me with the reality of her words as she extends her heavy arms, seemingly to embrace us all.

"Who is it?" my mother asks, a tinge of sadness clouding her joy as my father rises immediately from his favourite chair, a wry look in his dark eyes.

Aunt Rashna smiles, her lips oily with the news. "His name is Lachman Ramsingh. His parents are deceased, but his father and I attended service at the same temple. He is thirty-three and has never been married, and he works in the office of a hospital in Bombay. He wants to get into medicine."

I feel faint and need air, but Aunt Rashna comes closer.

"Look, Kamla, I have his photo. This is your future husband."

I wonder how I haven't noticed the large eight-by-ten photograph she clutches so tightly in her pudgy fingers, held high for all to see. I pray that no one can read my face, for surely my disappointment shows. There is no doubt about it. Lachman Ramsingh is hideous. His eyes are like small black marbles, his nose is an embarrassing hook that drifts southward over a small black caterpillar moustache, and he hardly has any hair on his conical head.

"What do you think?" my mother asks, her eyes darting to me and my father.

"He's ugly and I don't want to marry him!" I blurt suddenly.

"Watch your mouth!" my father shouts, blue veins standing at his throat as he angrily slams his fist against the mantelpiece, sending our family photos tottering into a heap. "We could not do better than getting into the Ramsingh family. You are past your prime, so stop this foolishness at once!"

"Kamla seems to think she's a Canadian!" Aunt Rashna interjects, her kohl-circled eyes as dark as chestnuts, her arms akimbo.

My mother doesn't say a word. Instead, she inspects the fallen photographs and runs her thin fingers along the mantel as though that action alone will set things right.

"As I was saying," Aunt Rashna continues, "look at Kamla, wearing jeans and scoop-necked tops! In Bombay she would have to wear a proper sari. None of this nonsense! And look at her hair. She needs a style to reflect something more Eastern. I don't approve of hair being allowed to hang loose. It is a reflection of our morals. She will have to change all that when she is Lachman's wife! He would not stand for it! You are Indian, my girl, and don't forget it!"

"But I'm Canadian. I was born here," I say softly, fully aware that, thanks to Aunt Rashna's shouts, no one is listening.

That evening, when all the others are in bed, I telephone my friend Gita. She is younger than I am and is already married with a small child. She, too, entered into an arranged marriage.

The house is deathly still, but in my mind Aunt Rashna's rage and her words still echo. "Gita," I whisper, "I have to be quick. They've found me a husband in Bombay and I don't know what to do."

Gita laughs huskily. "Go for it. It's an excellent chance to travel and have a man to love."

"Gita, I can do that without marrying this man."

"Look, I'm busy with the baby. It's like being a prisoner."

"But, Gita, how did you let a stranger into your heart, then, ultimately, into your bed?"

Gita laughs again. "Sundar was no stranger. My family knew him and I trust them. You should do the same. I must go. Little Garinder needs me."

After Gita hangs up, I think about what she said, but come to the conclusion that I shouldn't have expected her reaction to be different, since she, unlike myself, was born in India.

When I awake the next morning, it is grey, reflecting my emotions. No birds sing at the windows, and the house is a morgue. I wander into the kitchen and find a plate of samosas. I barely nibble at one before I feel constricted. My heart is as heavy as the day outside, and it seems as if the house I grew up in is no longer welcoming. On impulse I grab my jean jacket and go outside to my car. I want to drive into infinity, for there is no solution to the pain that gnaws in my stomach. Driving for perhaps an hour, putting the world on hold, I tell myself over and over that I can't marry Lachman Ramsingh. Eventually I pull into the parking lot of a McDonald's at King and Dufferin Streets, realizing I am thirsty.

I walk in just as breakfast ends and the Saturday-morning families begin dispersing. I am too dazed to notice when someone approaches me.

"Hi, Kamla," a voice says. I am more than surprised to see an old school friend, Bettina Hamilton. She and her twin brother, Andrew, and I attended grade school and high school together, though we lost touch in university. "Are you all right?" she asks, probably sensing my despair. "Come sit with us. Andrew's here. We should catch up."

Feeling like a rag doll, I walk toward the table Bettina points out and meet the icy blue blaze of Andrew's eyes, particularly noticeable set against his copper complexion. Glancing at Bettina, I see that, even as adults, the twins have maintained the high-cheekboned good looks of their childhood, as well as the tightly curled blondish hair that was attributed to their mixed black and white parentage. As I draw nearer, I see that Andrew's lush hair has grown into long, thick dreadlocks, paying homage, as it were, to the dark side of his family.

Seeing him sitting there awakens my childhood memories from deep slumber. I recall being in Grade Four when one of the bigger boys called me a "Paki" and I felt humiliated and ashamed. It was Andrew, with his blondish curls flying, who charged up angrily and confronted the boy. "If you call her that again," he said fiercely, "you'll have to deal with my fists!" The boy slunk away, and no one called me names after that.

And here Andrew is all these years later—the same look in his eyes, his smile ever challenging.

"Hi, Kamla," he says, standing to greet me. "Can I get you something?"

I tell him I have only come in to get a Diet Coke, but he insists on treating me. Snatching covert looks at him, I notice how he towers over his sister, his long legs filling his blue jeans nicely.

"I'm engaged," Bettina confides the moment Andrew leaves the table. "Remember Kevin Chang from our debating class? He's in law school now."

"I remember him. Congratulations." My mind wanders into the past in a vain attempt to forget the present. "And what about Andrew?" I hear myself asking.

She smiles. "Oh, you know him. He's still a favourite with all the girls. Just look at him. And how about you? Have you found someone special?"

Bettina's words bring me full tilt into the present. My eyes filling with tears, I can't help telling her about the impending arranged marriage. By the time Andrew returns to the table, I am more clearheaded, but my eyes betray me.

"What's wrong?" he asks.

All I am able to do is nod at Bettina, who relays everything I told her.

"What can I do to help?" Andrew asks

I dry my eyes with a couple of tissues and try to smile. "It's all right," I say feebly. "It probably won't be as bad as I first thought."

Bettina squeezes my palm. "Call me if you ever need to talk. I have to go. Kevin's meeting me to go shopping for antiques in Parkdale. It's good to see you. I mean it, call."

She scribbles her number on a scrap of paper, which I absently stuff into my jean jacket. As she walks away, I notice her long, easy strides, her curls bouncing. She is filled with joy, I think. Joy that I am missing out on.

"What are you thinking?" Andrew asks, staring intently at me.

"I was thinking about reality."

"What are your plans for the rest of the day? If you aren't busy, I was wondering if you'd like to take a walk down by the lakeshore."

I don't answer right away, perhaps because my thoughts are still in turmoil, and I know it will take more than a walk on a chilly morning to find solutions. My first instinct is to decline his offer, so I thank him. But as I turn away, I catch his eye and see his disappointment, so I change my mind.

The day doesn't warm up, but for the longest while Andrew and I sit in blissful silence on a wooden bench, our backs to the city, looking over the dark lake, the sky heavy with clouds.

"It's nice here," I say. "The breeze, the boats, even the hungry seagulls."

Andrew smiles. "I come here often. I have relatives in Ireland who are fishermen, and I feel something of their love of the sea here. Water must live in me."

Long after the noonday sun finally appears, Andrew and I rise from our roost and head for our cars.

"I'll call you," he says, his heavy hair glinting in the sunlight.

"I'll call," I add quickly, remembering the upheaval his call could cause at home.

My absence on a Saturday morning doesn't go unnoticed. Tension is thick in the air at home.

"You should have been here to help with lunch," my mother scolds as though I am still a child. "You know full well Aunt Rashna's here as a guest."

"Where were you?" my father shouts. "What could be more important than family prayers and sharing a meal!"

"I was with friends. I'm sorry to be late. I lost track of time," I say, removing my jacket.

"Did you also lose track of saying your prayers?" Aunt Rashna yells, coming into the room.

"God is always in my thoughts," I retort, sweeping past her to climb the stairs to my room. I can hardly breathe and can still hear Aunt Rashna's fussing downstairs.

"We have to get the wedding ornaments," she says briskly to my parents. "She'll settle down once things are in place."

☙

Andrew isn't home on Monday afternoon when I call in desperation from the St. George subway station. I have no choice but to leave a message, one that includes my telephone number. Maybe he won't call back, I tell myself, convinced I shouldn't worry.

"Give your mother a hand in the kitchen," my father says the moment I get home. "After dinner we can all pray for the success of your marriage."

My mother is already hard at work in the kitchen. She has made tandoori chicken, basmati rice, and fish in Madras sauce. Without looking up, she hands me the ingredients to make a salad.

"Where's Aunt Rashna?" I ask.

"She's gone to inquire about all the things you'll need for your wedding. We should be so grateful she's taken on this task for us."

After I do the salad, I roll out dough and make a dozen rotis with potatoes and lentils, already prepared by my mother. We work side by side as in the old days, and then the telephone rings and the bottom falls out of my stomach. I hear my father cross the floor to answer it. I can't hear his words and feel faint with anticipation. Then I hear him coming toward the kitchen and I tense, expecting a blow of some sort, expecting a hurricane in his eye, but he is smiling!

"That was Aunt Rashna," he says. "She'll be late for dinner and says we must go ahead, but put hers aside. She managed to get a wonderful sari for you, Kamla, and special henna to paint your hands before the wedding."

I paste a smile on my face, even though I sense the avalanche is picking up speed. Then the telephone rings again, and I rush past my father, but not without noticing the surprise in my mother's eyes. It is Andrew! There is no privacy. I try to prevent my voice from travelling all the way to the kitchen without having to whisper, but it is impossible.

"I want to see you," Andrew says, causing blood to rush to my head as I hold on to the telephone table for support. Then, without warning, something wild and adventurous takes hold of me and I can't stop myself.

"That's good," I say. "I can get that done." Andrew must be stunned. "I need to buy her a gift at Dufferin Mall at about 7:30. Yes, near the Wal-Mart entrance."

Andrew catches on, as I hoped, just as my mother's voice drifts into the room, heavy with her spices.

"Where are you going again, Kamla?"

I carefully replace the receiver in its cradle, barely able to conceal a smile. "I'm going to buy a bottle of wine for Aunt Rashna. It's my way of thanking her for all she's doing."

"But we already have liquor in the house," my father says, coming from the kitchen with one of my rotis in hand.

I force a smile. "I know," I say, meeting his eye, his accusing stare. "But this will be my own personal gift, so it will be different."

Andrew and I go immediately to the liquor store. I buy a bottle of pale pinkish wine he recommended, then we sit on one of the many crowded mall benches. There are people everywhere, but we manage to speak briefly.

"How's it at home?" he asks.

"It's worse," I reply. "My aunt has started buying things for the occasion."

For a long time Andrew doesn't say anything, and his eyes seem distant as he swallows hard. "Your husband will be a lucky man. Do you know I've always thought of you as an enigma? You've always been different from all the others. But in a good way, I mean. When's the guy coming?"

"In two months. Then I suppose it'll be off to Bombay for me, and goodbye to Toronto, but I don't want to go. You know that, don't you?"

"What a shame," Andrew says, his broad hands lying solidly on his lap, his eyes staring ahead unseeingly. "Perhaps I should really show you the city before you have to leave it."

"Andrew, I was born here. I already know the city."

"I know. I was trying to think of some way to postpone what's to come. I was trying to find an excuse to spend time together to help you forget your pain."

"Andrew, you're very kind, and I don't see why I shouldn't take you up on your offer."

It is a chilly afternoon in Queen's Park when I see Andrew again. He is standing beside a statue of a Native carved with heart-stopping elegance and power.

"Magnificent, isn't it?" Andrew says, his dreadlocks flowing in the cool wind.

For a moment I am not sure if he is talking about his locks or the Native, and I chuckle. "It's amazingly powerful. I wish I could draw strength from it."

Andrew looks at me with eyes that register double meanings.

"How's Bettina's wedding plans going?" I ask.

He laughs. "There are more plans than I can tell you. Every day Bettina and our mother are on the phone calling to compare prices of halls, caterers, florists, and even churches. Time is already running out, she says, since the wedding is in six months or so. How about you? Is it the same?"

"It's not the same. Everything's being done for me. It seems all I have to do is show up."

"And what would happen if you didn't?"

"That's unthinkable."

For the next six weeks Andrew and I meet after classes every day. I see it as an escape not only from the wedding plans, but also from Aunt Rashna who, as the time draws closer to Lachman's arrival, grows more sarcastic and cruel.

"I have had better curried prawns in the slums of Calcutta!" she tells me hastily, leaving the table after one of my finest meals. "Lachman will have to take you in hand. You cook like a Canadian, as if you're afraid of spices!"

I grow comfortable in Andrew's company, and for the first time in a long while I feel a part of things as he relates his family history. He tells me how his Irish grandparents disapproved of his parents' mixed marriage, and how they came around when the twins were born. He speaks of his uncle and aunt in the West Indies who are both teachers, and how much he admires them. Then he tells me about his strong working-class relations in Ireland, whom he resembles, and who barely make a living from the sea. I begin to look forward to his stories, his reassurance, and his laughter. Then one day we are walking near City Hall and a car draws up beside us. It is my father! He rolls down his car window angrily, his face dark with rage, his fists at the ready.

"What are you doing here, Kamla?" he shouts. "Get in the car! Have you forgotten you're engaged? It's a disgrace. You shouldn't be seen around town with a man."

"Dad," I say, trying to calm him, "this is Andrew, Bettina's brother. Remember him from school? I'm not a child, Dad. I can choose my friends."

"Not a child!" he screams. "You are under parental supervision until your marriage! You've brought disgrace upon the family. Get in the car!"

Andrew, who has witnessed the encounter, comes abreast of me. "Mr. Persaud, this is my fault. I wanted to show Kamla City Hall before she leaves for Bombay."

"I know what you'd like to show her!" my father snarls, gripping the steering wheel, teeth bared. "Get in the car, Kamla, before I drag you in."

Obeying my father, I am so humiliated that I can barely meet Andrew's eyes.

"Be on your way and leave my daughter alone!" my father shouts out the window, but Andrew stands firm. The car pulls away from the curb with a squeal, but I manage to glimpse Andrew in the rearview mirror. He looks stunned, hurt, and angry, but I don't miss it when he blows a kiss directly at me. I smile at his audacity.

"You're going to be confined to your room," my father says. "I see you have to be treated like a child. There are to be no phone calls and no visitors until you're respectably married. I won't stand for this kind of behaviour." He smashes his fist into the dashboard, then drives in silence. Glumly I know I'll still have to deal with my mother and Aunt Rashna's anger when I get home.

Lachman Ramsingh stays at the Holiday Inn and spends his evenings in our company. I am not allowed to be with him unchaperoned, but see him at meals and at prayer.

My future husband is nothing like I expected, what with his robust laugh and wonderful smile that brightens his cheeks. I can't help liking him. He was educated in England and is quite Westernized, much to Aunt Rashna's dismay.

Lachman is unaware that I am being confined to my room. He doesn't know that in his absence my father has taken to locking me up. However, one evening when my mother and Aunt Rashna are out shopping, a frantic telephone call comes. It is Aunt Rashna. My mother has suffered a dizzy spell and had to be taken to the hospital. Aunt Rashna insists that my father come downtown immediately.

My father, though shaken, still has the presence of mind to send me to my room, then locks the door. He offers Lachman no explanation, but leaves the key in his charge, telling him to remain in the house until he returns, and not to open my door except in an emergency.

I hear my father's car as it purrs down the driveway. Then I hear soft footsteps on the stairs. It is Lachman.

"Kamla," he says gently, "I'm going to let you out. You can go back in before your father gets back."

I can't believe my ears!

"Why is your father doing this?" he asks as the door swings open. His face is full of compassion, and I feel regret for all the negative thoughts I have had about him.

"It's a long story, Lachman."

"Tell me," he coaxes.

So, looking into his thickly lashed brown eyes, I tell him about my opposition to the arranged marriage, about Andrew and how my father saw us walking together.

Lachman knits his dark brows. "I had no idea. But it sounds to me that you and Andrew were getting close. I'm sorry, so very sorry."

"I miss him very much, but Dad's forbidden me to contact him."

"Would you like to call him?"

"I promised Dad I wouldn't."

"I'm not your father, but as your prospective husband, I give you permission. Be quick."

I punch out Andrew's number, my heart racing, praying that he will answer, and he does. "Andrew," I croak, "it's Kamla."

"Kamla, are you all right? Are you married?"

"No."

"What's the guy like?"

"He's nicer than I thought."

"Well, I guess this is it then. Is this the part where I wish you good luck?"

"Wait, Andrew, I want to see you. How about the St. George subway entrance tomorrow at 2:30?"

I race up the stairs, where Lachman waits patiently. He

smiles and rises from his chair. "Now I have the difficult task of locking you in again," he says. "But before I do I want to let you know that you're the most beautiful woman I've ever laid eyes on. You'll surely make a wonderful wife."

Andrew is waiting at the subway. He looks deep in thought, but when he sees me coming, he smiles. "Kamla," he shouts, holding out his arms, and I bury my face in his broad shoulders, tears stealing down my cheeks. "I love you!" he whispers, but I am too frightened to reply.

I tear out of his arms and run down the subway stairs.

"Kamla!" he cries. "Come back!"

During my mother's three days in the hospital, I am unable to visit her. My father prevents me from going, so I am pleased to hear that arrangements are being made to have her home the next day. But my happiness is darkly stained, since her return will also speed up the wedding date.

That night, after being dutifully locked in my room, my father and Aunt Rashna leave for the hospital as usual. I sit in my room, waiting for Lachman's footsteps on the stairs, but all is silent. Then I hear his muffled voice and know he is on the telephone. Half an hour passes before he finally approaches as softly as a Bengal tiger.

"Kamla," he whispers, "pack an overnight bag. I'll help you."

"Are we going out?" I ask, sounding foolish.

"No," he replies quietly, "you are." He opens the door and stands across from me, smiling with sheer satisfaction. "I've been talking to your friend Andrew."

My eyes open wide in surprise.

"No questions now," he says, raising a firm finger to his lips.

"I found his number on your pillow the other night and I memorized it."

"What did you say to him?"

"That's not important right now. What is important is that you hurry. Andrew will meet you in twenty minutes at the McDonald's at King and Dufferin. He mentioned Niagara Falls and wants to spend the rest of his life with you. I know now that he loves you and I feel that you love him, too."

I can't believe what I am hearing. Here is a chance that may never come again. Impulsively I hug Lachman in gratitude.

"I do love him!" I confess through tears.

"Hurry then! Don't worry about your father and aunt. I'll deal with them. I should have been honest before and let it be known that I only agreed to this marriage because I love someone else."

"How's that?" I ask, seeing sadness cloud his eyes as I stare at him in confusion.

"I'm bisexual. You marrying me would have made me respectable in Bombay. But it wouldn't have been fair to you. I've been in love with an Englishman for years, a man who loves me, too, and has been patiently waiting. I have finally, in these past few days, decided to risk my reputation and my career to join him at last in England."

I am not sure what Lachman is thinking as he waits for my father, not sure what he will say. My heart bleeds for him, and my hope is that he will find his happiness. But I know that once I am with Andrew, nothing my parents or Aunt Rashna can say will touch me. I will be far away from their rage, and I know that with the thought of Andrew waiting, Andrew, whom I adore, I already feel as if I am driving through red lights.

Remembering Serge

*M*r. Holgate was certainly the most handsome man my sister, Emma, and I had ever seen. Emma was seven and I was almost five when we first saw the large eight-by-ten photograph of this man and became mesmerized by his fair skin, dark brows, straight brown hair, and lips that smiled softly as though somewhat amused at our adoration. His was the face we conjured up when we listened to fairy tales about princes. Looking deep into the sepia photograph, we wondered why he had died. Had he been ill? Did he commit suicide? Was he murdered? Each imagined death made him slightly more intriguing than the last. Yet Mr. Holgate's face was also the one that haunted us in our childish games when we frightened each other silly by plunging rooms into darkness at night and running off screaming "Mr. Holgate is going to get you!" To be sure, Emma and I shared a love/hate relationship with the old photograph of a Canadian man we had never seen who had been the owner of Serge Island Estate where our father worked as the accountant.

Tucked away in the lush southeastern parish of St. Thomas, Serge Island was one of Jamaica's best-kept secrets.

❦

The members of my family were coloured Jamaicans of black, East Indian, Jewish, and Scottish extraction, and it was often said that my father, Edmund, resembled both of the popular political leaders of the time, Norman Manley and Alexander Bustamante, with his light brown skin, prominent forehead, and wavy hair. Most of the country locals called my father Baa Gee, perhaps because they were unable to pronounce our Portuguese-Jewish surname, Gabay, or because the nickname was short for Brother G.

Serge Island was a thriving sugar estate in the 1940s and had as a landmark its own Great House, a large Colonial-style home probably left over from slavery days when such an impressive building with its huge outdoor fountain complete with lily pads once belonged to affluent plantation owners. The sprawling house had seen its share of hard times and was now used for nothing more glamorous than offices for men like my father. There was something quite unsettling about that house, and without knowing exactly what it was, Emma and I and our other four siblings kept away from it.

Many families such as ours settled in Serge Island. Originally they came from other parishes and towns. In our case, both my parents were from Montego Bay, a much larger tourist town. The closest community to Serge was Morant Bay, made famous many years ago by a slave rebellion. But even with its shops, courthouse, police station, schools, and churches, it was hard to disguise the fact that Morant Bay was little more than a sleepy seaside village.

So isolated were we at Serge Island that Emma and I received our first education from tutors who were brought to our home on the estate to teach us the three Rs. Our long, hot days were spent in one of the small wooden cottages often used as servants' quarters. The cottages were just off the main house, and it was here that we used slates and slate pencils to laboriously scribble school work within full view of a garden bright with hibiscuses, roses, and chrysanthemums.

How we longed, though, to chase "needle cases," or dragon-flies, and watch ants in their nests as Edward, one of our older brothers did. How wonderful it would have been to run with the sunlight on our cheeks in pursuit of butterflies.

Only a stone's throw from our house, just past the old cooper shop and stables, the green forests began. Here the fragrance of the cool, rushing river was pungent, and its call was almost as strong as our mother's voice.

Our older sister, Cherie, and two of our older brothers went to schools outside Serge. Douglas, the eldest, whom we called John, was about thirteen and away at boarding school in Kingston. So, too, for that matter was Cherie, who was nearly fourteen. Our brother, David, who was eleven, went to a small village school with ten-year-old Edward.

It was with our brothers that Emma and I explored the river-banks. We learned how to set traps for janga and other shellfish, and even how to keep our clothes dry by rolling them up to our waists so that our parents would not know we had been to the forbidden river. Instinctively we avoided the silent pools that looked as inviting as lagoons. It was there, overhung with tangled vines, that the river was deepest and most dangerous.

On weekends we usually explored the river's secret mean-derings, where tall trees edged its banks and the forest floor was thickly carpeted in ferns, watergrass, and vines. High above us the air was rife with bird song, for cling-clings, pitcharies, Auntie Katies, and banana beenies were on the wing, unmindful of us and our two dogs, Kitch and Betty.

When David, too, went off to boarding school in Kingston,

Emma and I were left to the devices of Edward, or Teddy, as we called him. Teddy was fearless and impulsive. Once, the local vet, who lived approximately eight miles from us, mentioned in casual conversation with my father that he was thinking of giving us a couple of pet chickens. Teddy overheard and, when two days passed and the chickens had still not come, he decided that we three children would have to get them ourselves. We didn't tell a soul about our plans. Mama would have been worried sick, especially since we didn't have a phone. We must have walked for hours, past tall cane fields, banana groves, and wild bush along a lonely gravel-strewn road.

As it turned out, the vet was more than surprised to see us arrive with the setting sun. He gave us a warm meal, then drove us home safely, extracting a promise from us never to do such a thing again. And as a little bonus he gave each of us a chicken.

❦

Emma enjoyed climbing; she was better at it than most boys, being equally at home swinging from the aerial roots of a large banyan tree near our house as in the upper branches of wild guavas. She climbed anything she could and took me with her to the tops of our tall chicken coops, where in the late evenings we had an excellent view of the house and gardens, as well as a ringside seat to the haunting golden sunsets that one can only see in the Jamaican countryside. Up there, in our castle in the clouds, Emma and I would talk about everything, such as why so many people were called John. First, there was our brother, then there was John the postman, John the cowcart man, and John the barber. How amazing, we thought.

It was there on our perch that Emma had the idea of sending a package of hot red peppers to Cherie in Kingston, since boarding-school food, we figured, was probably bland. And furthermore, what did American nuns know about Jamaican cooking? It took us hours to find enough ripe bird peppers to fill a shoe box. And with none of the servants or the gardener knowing what we were up to, the excitement became even more intense. Eventually the box was wrapped with string and brown paper, and Mama promised to mail it for us. We never knew if the peppers ever reached their destination, since what really mattered to us was the pleasure in organizing it all.

Our absent sister and brothers usually came home for the holidays. One year my brother, John, and a friend, plus the gardener, decided to go off into the bush to find a tree suitable for Christmas. David wanted to go with them, but at first they said no, considering him too little. However, after a lot of pleading, he was reluctantly taken along. As it turned out, that was fortunate, since John had a serious accident with the sharp cutlass. It was young David who removed his own shirt and used it as a temporary bandage and tourniquet on his brother's blood-soaked hand, which required many stitches. David's gallant act more than forty years ago is still spoken about today in family legend.

All of us had many adventures during those idyllic days in Serge Island. Certainly our parents were not aware when we slipped out at night to chase fireflies, and they surely did not know that we often explored the empty sugar factory long after a horn called the *kauchi* was blown at the end of the day to signal closing. We were oblivious to danger even when my brothers loaded us onto empty railway carts and, with a hefty push, sent us careering and screaming with delight down an abandoned track.

My father bought a piece of property in St. Thomas. He named it Beckideed, using the first letters of our names. It was nothing more than rugged bush with no real dwelling to speak of. We children loved it, of course, but my mother did not; she found it primitive and forbidding.

Once, when we were exploring there, we children got separated and I found myself in the company of Cherie, who was unfamiliar with the bush. Without warning she fell into a deep pit. It had likely been dug by locals and camouflaged with tree branches to trap small animals.

Finding my five-year-old self alone above the pit was a frightening experience, even though sunlight still slanted through the trees and the air was alive with bird song. Fear got the better of me, and I made a reckless decision. With a flying leap, I joined my sister in her prison, much to her annoyance.

Time passes slowly when one is confined. The interior of that pit still haunts my mind: the dry, loose soil, the jagged stones, the small, coiled insects, the ants, and the snails that left silver trails. At ground level, above us, we occasionally heard the rustling of leaves and wondered if the sound indicated the presence of lizards, snakes, or perhaps a mongoose. Fortunately for us, rescue eventually came, for farm labourers working close by heard our shouts.

Our worst nightmares came when servants told us ghost stories. They spoke of beasts they called "rolling calves," ghost bulls on chains who tore around houses at night, wreaking havoc. Then there was the "three foot horse," a giant ghost horse with three legs who prowled the night. The servants said that the only way to prevent these ghosts from haunting us was to have someone in the house leave a Bible open with a skeleton key placed on the open pages. Since we never saw any of these demons, we assumed someone in the house was doing the Bible trick. But there is an old family legend that when my brother, John, was about three, he talked about having three friends who came and played in his room at night. No one took him seriously. Then, one evening, my mother said she had a dream in which a long-dead family friend came and told her never to leave the baby's window ajar at night, not even a crack. On investigating, some old servants who had been at the house long before our family even came to live there, told her to be careful, for just outside my brother's window there was a raised mound they said was used as a burial place for babies during slavery days. They insisted that was probably where my brother's "friends" had come from.

Eventually we moved from that house to another in Serge Island, which we still refer to as the "new house," even though it was, in fact, old. At that house Emma and I grew closer, being the last of the children at home. We grew wilder and freer among our animals—two cows, Maggie and Billy, plus goats, rabbits, guinea pigs, dogs, cats, and chickens. We dug our heels in and continued to climb trees, set calabans, and hunt lizards and dragonflies in a virtual race against the inevitability of growing up.

In the end, though, our family, like many others, left Serge. We heard it said that the economy steered my father's hand to a "better life" in Kingston.

None of us have returned to Serge. We guard the memory of it like a precious jewel. It was a place where we truly felt free, a place forever caught in sepia like the pale eyes of Mr. Holgate.

Roberta on the Beach

How far the distance from a childhood of poverty in the blazing tropical sun to where I stand today, a creative young man equally at home with pen or brush, defiant of raging snows that whistle and sting, even as I write, pressed against a frosty window, determined to capture the essence of a past that haunts me. My pen wields tears like ink and guides my hand as creases in my brow awaken wells of remembering. I recall her well, Roberta, my beloved sister, the enigmatic subject of my painting *Roberta on the Beach*.

—Caleb Douglas

*T*he way some people thought you would expect everyone from Montego Bay to be either lucky or rich. This was probably due to the town's location on the picturesque

Jamaican north coast where many of the locals benefitted from a thriving tourist industry.

It was in this supposedly idyllic setting that Roberta Douglas was born. She was not representative of those who were indeed lucky or rich. Her family was part of what might be termed the working poor. Roberta herself felt hard done by and often wore an expression of defiance on her otherwise attractive face.

When she was sixteen, she would sashay down the main street with an air of affluence. It was a game she enjoyed playing. After all, who was to know that her bright clothes were mainly hand-me-downs? No one looking at her noticed her clothes first, anyway; it was her long reddish hair, pale, lightly tanned complexion, and startling green eyes that grabbed attention. Even more of a curiosity was the fact that her brothers and sisters were all black.

Like most Jamaicans, Roberta could trace her ancestors to various origins, in her case, Scottish, Jewish, and African. Roberta's looks were said to be like those of the Scottish great-grandmother on her father's side of the family. Her father, George Douglas, was the son of a Scottish immigrant named Trevor Douglas, who came to the island in the late 1800s. Eventually he married a local woman named Edith Oliver. Edith was from a long line of proud black Jamaicans with impressive full lips, broad nose, brown eyes, and short-cropped curly hair. It was an ideal marriage; Trevor delighted in Edith's simple ways, and she in his sophistication. Unfortunately Edith had never been a strong woman and was plagued by epileptic seizures. She conceived a child, and because of improper medical care, only lived to see him reach his first year.

Trevor, a young man of twenty-four, resigned himself to raising the child on his own and eventually broke all ties with his homeland. He was a devoted father who saw to his son George's education and care, and he lived to see his child grow up to marry a local girl named Hannah Weiss, delighting in the birth of six of their children. George, a self-taught accountant, took on freelance work to supplement his family's income. Employment was scarce, and the home was often reduced to the most meagre fare. Hannah, a handsome woman of Jewish and black descent, wore her long black hair in a coil down her back. She was good-humoured and sympathetic and expected the best of others. And, although it was a financial hardship, she took in occasional washing to make sure her children were educated.

Roberta, the eldest girl, often spent her days at Cornwall Beach, a popular tourist haunt, where she sat and listened to foreigners converse about their faraway homelands. For Roberta, names such as Helsinki, Copenhagen, Glasgow, and Hammersmith became an enchantment. She would close her eyes, dig her toes deep into the sand, and let her imagination take her to unexplored worlds where neither the sea, nor the salty breeze, nor the cry of wandering seabirds could disturb her reverie. But it seemed to her that all too soon she would have to return to the reality of scarcity and the cramped cottage with its pathetic cardboard walls, creaking floors, and crooked windows. She could hardly remember a time when she hadn't slept three to a bed. It was much the same for the others, since her parents shared one room. Slim and Caleb, her older brothers, shared another, and she and her sisters, Sheila, Georgina, Elaine, Lorraine, and Maggie, shared two rooms where double beds in each room restricted movement. The tiny living room offered the only respite, but it was really part of the kitchen where there seemed to be a constant stream of family.

The cottage's location just outside town was an excellent one. It overlooked the blue Caribbean Sea from a rocky perch. At the time of its original purchase by Roberta's now-deceased grandfather, Trevor, arid land such as theirs was considered to be of little value and therefore a poor investment. It was with much foresight on his part that Trevor still went ahead and bought the land with the cottage on it, even though he couldn't afford to replace the dilapidated building.

Roberta could remember running along the rocky pathway

in front of the cottage, catching the wind in her hair, tasting the expected sharpness of salt in her mouth, and hearing the rhythmic call of the sea. As a child, she chased butterflies in the sunshine and hunted fireflies during the long evenings. The ever-watchful Hannah would wring her hands in constant fear that one of her children might fall from the treacherous path into the swirling sea below, and was grateful that it never happened.

For Roberta's eighteenth birthday the family held a modest celebration: a virtual feast of cake, ginger beer, rice and peas, and chicken. Even Roberta, who was usually discontented with what the household had to offer, had to admit that this was a fine celebration, which was not only for her birthday, but also for her graduation from high school.

Long into the night, when the rest of the family had retired to bed, Roberta lay awake, contemplating her future. She felt unfulfilled. Slim and Caleb had recently started work in one of the local hotels, but their salaries weren't nearly enough to offer any security. If her Grandpa Trevor were alive, she thought, there would be no cause for uncertainty.

She lay rigid in the shared bed where, being closest to the window, she had a good view of the cliffs outside. She could see where the land, like a pointing finger, jutted into the sea. She could have easily been mesmerized by its beauty, but hushed whispers from the living room reeled her in like a hooked fish, and with a jolt, she returned to the reality of the cramped bed.

Reluctantly she turned her head away from the beckoning horizon, her ears straining to hear the whispered conversation. It was her mother and father. Never did night noises seem louder to her. The rattling of the wooden window frame in the night breeze was an annoyance, the buzzing of insects a discordance, and the sea quarrelling with the rocks below deafened her.

"She might not want to go," her mother whispered.

There was a long silence before her father answered. "Hannah, she'll want to go. She'll be right at home over there. Haven't you noticed how she craves the company of the tourists?"

Noticing how sure of himself her father sounded, Roberta sat bolt upright. "Papa!" she called out as if in warning, swinging her bare legs over the side of the bed. The hushed whispers died as she steadied herself beside the open door, heart racing. "Is something wrong?"

Her father looked up wearily, fixing his eyes on her startled face. "Sit down, Roberta." As Hannah patted him gently on the shoulder, he smiled weakly. "We were talking about you."

"Yes, Roberta, your father and me have news. I got a letter from your Aunt Melanie. Is my older sister who go away to England as a domestic but become big businesswoman."

"What's happened to Aunt Melanie?" Roberta asked.

"Nothing happen," her mother replied. "But out of the blue Melanie write and offer something too good to be true. She want to educate one of you children in England. Slim and Caleb like their jobs at the hotel, so we think of you since you the oldest girl. Aunt Melanie think one of the family might be interested in nursing."

A thin sweat broke out on Roberta's pale forehead. She felt faint. She clutched at the edges of a stool to steady herself. Her throat was so dry she could barely speak. Imagine, a chance to go to England, she thought. She didn't much care for nursing, but she would have agreed to anything that offered a way out. Her green eyes blazed in the darkness. "Papa," she whispered, "it's what I've always wanted."

It took six months for all the arrangements to be finalized. There were long lineups in the passport office, a passport photograph to be taken, and a suitable person found to sign the documents. Hannah mentioned their need for clothes at the local church. Roberta would have died of shame had she known, but she was so caught up in the excitement of the planning that much of the details washed over her.

At Montego Bay Airport the rest of the family were full of concerns: Would she be warm enough? Why was the plane so small? Would Aunt Melanie be able to recognize her? Roberta brushed aside their fears; like a racehorse, she strained for the excitement of the race.

Hannah clung to her only momentarily and hid her swollen eyes behind her long black hair. And her father squeezed her hand so tightly it felt like the embrace of a shackle.

"You're the first one to go," he said gruffly. "Try to help out the others. Don't be like my father who never looked back to his homeland and family. Roberta, we love you." With a final squeeze of his daughter's hand, he shuffled over to Hannah's side, feeling like an old man, and reached with trembling fingers for his wife's steady grip as his green eyes swam with unshed tears.

"Hannah, my darling," he said, "I have the strangest feeling I will never see Roberta again."

Hannah arched her brows and pursed her full lips to silence him. "Don't be silly, George. She be back. It's your Scottish blood make you so superstitious."

In spite of her reassurances, Hannah's heart skipped a beat. She feared George's prediction, since on more than one occasion in the past he had been right. He wasn't wrong this time, either, for less than a year after Roberta's departure, he succumbed to a fatal heart attack. The family was devastated, and Roberta was immediately notified. Slim and Caleb suddenly found themselves responsible for the rest of the family, and they made sure Roberta remained in England. Aunt Melanie saw the wisdom in this decision, realizing that her niece's interest in nursing was flagging and any break from the program could spell the end of it.

In England Roberta felt like an orchid in an igloo. Nothing could have prepared her for the incessant damp and cold. Layers and layers of clothing were never enough to alleviate her constant shivering. But by sheer determination she swore she would accustom herself to the weather, just as she accommo-dated herself to living in her aunt's home with the modern conveniences of hot running water and a proper living room with a television. She even had her own bedroom and full run of the rest of the house. Aunt Melanie's brisk, efficient, organized manner impressed Roberta, though. It was so unlike her mother's easygoing ways and ready laugh. Time and again, Roberta missed the closeness of home, and couldn't help but wonder if her formidable aunt, who appeared to be such a tower of strength, might have a softer side.

For Roberta, London was overwhelming, with its churches, castles, monuments, shops, crowds, double-decker buses, and the Underground. There were days when she would wrap herself in her warmest blanket and watch television by the fire for most of the day, but Aunt Melanie would subtly steer her back to her studies.

After the news of her father's death, Roberta pretended that life for her hadn't existed before going to England. In doing so, she shut off the harsh realities in the lives of those left at home, and decided not to write her family or read their letters.

Because of shyness, she had, at first, remained aloof from her fellow students, but eventually she began to study in the student lounge where a number of her colleagues gathered. One of them, Suleika Ramsaroop, a bright, friendly girl from Bombay, introduced Roberta to her circle of friends.

One day, when Roberta was immersed in conversation with students from Malaysia and Burma, a pleasant Scottish burr attracted her attention. It sounded so much like Grandpa Trevor's that she caught her breath sharply and saw, framed in the doorway, a tall blond young man with blue eyes. He came over to where she was and introduced himself. His name was Chester Daley, a doctor from Scotland.

During the next few weeks, Chester and Roberta struck up a close friendship. Aunt Melanie quickly became accustomed to his presence in her home. She watched with mixed feelings as her niece blossomed under the ever-watchful eye of the young doctor and knew without doubt that the two young people were falling in love.

Melanie Weiss had never married or had children, and now, in her late fifties, looked back with much regret at the chances she had missed. She recognized in Roberta a certain sassiness that she herself had possessed as a young girl and hoped her niece wouldn't make the same mistakes she had made. Being a regular churchgoer and a well-respected member of the black community, Aunt Melanie was surprised when Chester, after six months, instead of proposing marriage, suggested that Roberta and he move in together.

Roberta felt mature enough to make her own decisions, therefore she and Chester found themselves a flat close by. Aunt Melanie's only demand was that Roberta not give up her studies, not realizing that she had nothing to fear on that account because, under Chester's guidance, Roberta buckled down to her training.

Roberta's new home was a small flat with a tiny fireplace and only four rooms to move around in, but with Chester beside her, it felt like a palace. Her mail was forwarded from Aunt Melanie's place and quickly, without being read, became fuel for her fireplace. Her life was too perfect to be interrupted by the sadness and depression of those across the ocean.

Aunt Melanie remained a part of their lives. Sunday-afternoon visits with her became a ritual. Chester, too, enjoyed the roast beef, rice and peas, and hot hams she always seemed to have on the table. Her thirty years in England hadn't diminished her preference for Jamaican food.

As time passed, Chester's letters to his parents in Scotland were more frequently punctuated with the names of Roberta and Aunt Melanie. As a result, his parents grew impatient to meet the girl who had won their son's heart.

It was inevitable that Roberta would eventually see Scotland, the land of her ancestors. She had long decided on this, even before meeting Chester. Now, with his encouragement, they immersed themselves in travel brochures and plans to visit his homeland.

They decided to take the train. Roberta was as restless as a puppy, and even three suitcases weren't enough to hold her down. But on the train she sat glued to the window, observing the landscape flash by mile after mile as she held tightly to Chester's hand.

She thought it was magical when they crossed the Scottish border. To her, it was destiny fulfilled. She strained her ears to hear distant bagpipes and church bells, and in her elation imagined she did.

She was fascinated with her surroundings: heather-covered hills, meadows, fields, castles around every bend, and countless herds of sheep, all of which set her blood racing. She wasn't at all prepared for the surprise of Chester's parents' country estate. By estate standards, it was only modest, but for Roberta it might as well have been Tara in *Gone with the Wind*. It was called Hawthorne Hold and was set amid rolling green hills and a well-tended garden. The Daleys, broad-minded and middle-aged, welcomed Roberta with open arms, and she, who had never been inside a home such as theirs, was quick to compliment all its finery.

Mrs. Daley showed them to their rooms and somehow managed to keep out of their way until suppertime, giving Chester ample time to escort Roberta around the estate and point out things he remembered fondly. First, they explored the grounds and what must at one time have been stables, then they wandered in the small woods behind the property and later investigated the lush garden.

Once back inside the main building, they settled in the parlour. Mr. Daley popped in just as they were catching their breath and offered them both a nip of Scotch to welcome them. The shaggy-haired gentleman seemed unassuming, but when he asked Roberta about her family and home in Jamaica, she felt self-conscious and determined not to disappoint him. Without anyone to contradict her, she effortlessly embroidered stories about her origins. Grandpa Trevor Douglas became a rich Scottish immigrant, her parents' little cottage became a villa, and even the rocky cove became an exclusive beach. She related half-truths about the closeness of her family, surprising even Chester.

That evening at supper, when Mrs. Daley mentioned over boiled cabbage and pot roast that their guest must be more accustomed to exotic and expensive food, Roberta hid her eyes behind her hair, a habit she had learned from her mother. She realized she had betrayed these good people and longed to escape. The remaining days of her visit couldn't pass quickly enough. Her silly game had ruined Scotland for her. Finally she convinced Chester to leave a day early.

After returning to London, she continued to ignore the many letters from home. Fear that her invented past would be exposed became an obsession. She immersed herself in study, becoming so self-absorbed that she hardly noticed on her regular Sunday visits to Aunt Melanie that her aunt was showing signs of physical weakness and seemed unable to cope with the house. She didn't even notice that the sparkle had gone from her aunt's smile.

Melanie Weiss had known for a long time about tumours, which at first appeared in her breasts and then spread to her lungs. She was well aware of her impending demise and, wanting to do something worthwhile for her sister, Hannah, had offered to help educate one of her children. She wasn't at all prepared for the great burst of love she felt for Roberta, and constantly chided herself for not confiding in anyone, especially Roberta, about the true state of her health. Nevertheless she trusted in the Lord that with Chester on the scene Roberta would be looked after.

Then, one weekend when the usual Sunday-dinner invitation didn't come by telephone, Roberta and Chester decided to visit Aunt Melanie, anyway. Roberta let herself into her aunt's house where silence met them, and it was evident that Aunt Melanie hadn't been there for days. Roberta used the phone to call the few friends of her aunt's she could remember, but came up with nothing. It wasn't until Chester ventured next door and made inquiries that a Mrs. Bowles from Trinidad and her family came forward with information. However, by the time they made it to the hospital, Aunt Melanie already had both feet planted in the next world.

Aunt Melanie's minister, the Reverend V. Robottom, officiated at the funeral on what Roberta felt to be a particularly cold and damp Wednesday morning. She was particularly moved by the many Londoners who came to pay their last respects to her aunt, the popular grocery store owner, and was grateful for the support of Chester's strong arms.

Aunt Melanie's will was read the following afternoon in the presence of a solicitor. Melanie Weiss proved more than generous, leaving her niece the tidy sum of twenty thousand pounds while proceeds from the sale of her home and business were to be given to her sister, Hannah Douglas. Hannah was, however, not to be informed of any of this until after the actual sale of the properties. In addition, many of Melanie's personal effects and furniture were to be donated to charity at Roberta's discretion. Afterward, Roberta spoke with the solicitor until well into the evening regarding these personal details and others, which she wished to be clarified.

For the next couple of days she spent her time sorting through her aunt's personal effects. Charity stood to gain considerably, since Roberta couldn't store the belongings elsewhere. She chose only to keep the mahogany dining-room table and chairs that she and Chester and her aunt had used so many times. The strain of these sad duties weighed heavily on her. She turned only to Chester for comfort, since she chose not to inform her mother about the recent death. So she hardly had time herself to recover from the initial shock when, while clearing out Aunt Melanie's house, she received a fateful phone call.

The call was long distance from Jamaica. Roberta's heart pounded uncontrollably. She calmed herself, assuming it might be a friend of her aunt's, but it was Roberta's younger sister, Elaine. The voice, sounding hauntingly familiar, crackled over the line. "Hello, Roberta, is that you? It's Elaine."

The lilt of the Jamaican accent sounded painfully quaint, and it caused childhood memories to flood through Roberta's mind.

"Roberta, are you still there? We haven't heard from you for so long that we decided to phone. I'm calling from a neighbour's house. We still don't have a phone."

Roberta gripped the receiver hard, feeling, on the one hand, comforted by the familiar voice, and on the other, embarrassed by its rustic intonations. Had she sounded like that? she wondered. "Is something wrong?" she finally asked out loud. "Has someone died?" All the while, she imagined Elaine at the other end of the line being impressed by her English accent, but Elaine replied so quickly that Roberta knew there was no time for her sister to fully absorb anything Roberta was saying.

"No one's dead, Roberta, but Mama's quite sick, and she wants you to come home."

Cheeks burning, Roberta bit her lips as her eyes brimmed with tears. "Did she hear about Aunt Melanie?"

"Hear what?"

"She died a week ago," Roberta said, not bothering to soften the blow since, after all, this was Elaine, who was as strong as an ox.

"What! Why didn't you call us?" Elaine demanded, an angry edge creeping into her voice.

Roberta sunk her nails into the flesh of her palm and lied her way out of the predicament. "Things were too busy here—ministers to see, solicitors, real-estate brokers, funeral directors to talk to, decisions to be made, and even teas."

"Did you do all that alone?" Elaine asked, sounding more sympathetic.

"Well," Roberta replied, "my boyfriend, Chester Daley, helped me, but mostly I did it alone."

"Roberta, you must come home, especially now. Mama is so ill. We're afraid of losing her, and now we can't even tell her about her sister. It would be too much of a shock."

Then and there Roberta decided to go home for a month. Aunt Melanie's passing had taken its toll on her, and she realized that the home from which she had shielded herself for so long had finally caught up with her.

Two days was all she had to wait for the departure. And when she told Chester of her plans, he was pleased, then surprised her by deciding to join her there after her first week with her family. Roberta was panic-stricken, trying to figure out how to explain away her fabricated stories.

Any amount of years away from home changes one's perspective of what home was really like, and Roberta, feeling more English than Jamaican, arrived on the island wearing a drab brown English summer dress, which was at odds with the vibrant colours of the island. She was surprised at the many changes around her. Her eldest brother, Slim, had shaken off the family nickname by becoming a strapping young man. And Caleb and her sisters were no longer children. But judging from their speech and well-worn clothes, Roberta imagined that nothing had happened in their lives. The thought of Chester among them terrified her, and a hot flush stained her cheeks with shame.

The cottage was smaller than she remembered, and much shabbier due to neglect. Even the garden seemed abandoned to weeds. She found her mother propped up in bed with two soft pillows. Roberta's impression was that Hannah had aged a hundred years, because her once-proud jaw looked slack and her lush black hair was streaked with white. Sobs escaped Roberta as she held her mother in her arms, then she suddenly released herself from the noose of her mother's caress and backed away from the sick bed.

"Chester will be coming next week," she said as her large, disappointed eyes swept the room.

Hannah read her thoughts. "You both can have this room," she said weakly. "I stay with the boys. It won't be for long." Her mother's simple solution brought another flush of shame. Roberta lowered her lashes, as if that action alone would prevent her mother noticing. But Hannah wasn't finished with her yet. "Why don't you tell me about my sister? Is Elaine who tell me. I know something wrong. What's the matter, girl? You forget where you come from?"

Roberta turned away in confusion. The problem wasn't in forgetting; it was in remembering.

Over the next few days Roberta went about the cottage with a critical eye. There were creaky floors, loose shingles, and lopsided window frames. Her vigilance, inevitably, got on the nerves of the rest of the family, with all her complaining. Nothing, as far as she was concerned, was as good as she had had in England. Sheila, Elaine, and Lorraine avoided her as best they could, then giggled behind her back at what they perceived as her phony accent, since Jamaicanisms were already creeping back into her speech. Maggie and Georgina had had enough, but felt compelled to be nice to her, since she had been away for so long. Slim and Caleb, who were out of the house for most of the day, were glad not to be directly involved in the quarrels. Only Hannah thrived in the tense atmosphere. It was as if the mere presence of Roberta caused her eyes to shine and her cheeks to glow as she endured the girl's complaints.

By the fourth day, a more relaxed Roberta decided to provide the family with some of the necessities they lacked. Juice glasses, guest towels, and cutlery were purchased with the intention of using them upon Chester's arrival. She hired a handyman for repairs and painting. She couldn't alter the actual size of the house before Chester's arrival and, to her dismay, realized that the washroom needed an overhaul, as well as the kitchen. But all she could do to cheer things up was to paint them in bright colours. In spite of her efforts, the thought of Chester's imminent arrival made her positively ill, because nothing went according to her plan. Her attempts to improve things began to feel like trying to stop Niagara Falls with a Band-Aid. There was no stopping the army of cockroaches that inhabited the house, and no matter how much was done, invariably, there was always something more. And then there was the garden...

The night before Chester's arrival, after clearing away things, Roberta was unable to sleep. She swung her feet over the side of the bed where her soft, downy English slippers awaited her. Unlike the night of her eighteenth birthday, there were no voices to disturb her; the rest of the household slept peacefully, unaware of her turmoil. A walk in the cool air could be just what she needed to calm her, for already there was a terrible knot in her stomach. She kicked off the slippers and padded softly across the uncarpeted floors, careful not to disturb anyone.

Only a drowsy Hannah detected her movements. She turned from her sleep, full of concern, and whispered softly in the silence, "That you, Roberta?"

Roberta felt years of pent-up resentment die in her throat. There was never any privacy at home. She should have known better. But somehow this time it felt good having someone near caring about her.

"Yes, Mama, it's me. I need some fresh air." She listened as her mother moaned softly and went back to sleep.

That night the wind was wild and raw. Roberta stepped out, and it greeted her with such fury that it whipped her light gown against her lean frame, revealing all that was fragile about her to the wicked night. She held tightly to her clothing and climbed down the well-remembered rocky path. The salty wind stung her eyes, almost blinding her, but she hurried on, impatient for the beach below where her toes would soon sink into the cool sand.

The beach was dark and deserted. There were no sounds except for the lapping of waves. Her feet were washed by the water, then her knees were covered. Before she knew it she was waist-deep. Feeling light-headed, she sang to herself and waded farther out into the darkness where the sea, like an ever-patient lover, waited in silence to receive her fully. Thrilled by the rushing water, she thought about Chester and raised her fist defiantly against the miles of ocean that separated them. She heard the urgent call of a lonely seabird, sensing its desolation.

In a moment of total abandon she imagined reaching out for Chester through the starlit water, offering no resistance when waves crashed around her, then closed furiously over her head.

❦

On the afternoon of Chester's arrival, brilliant sunshine lit the skies, and even the wind had dropped considerably, as though it, too, stood at attention. When the tall blond man with the friendly blue eyes arrived at Montego Bay Airport, a sense of festiveness was in the air. Throngs of local people awaiting relatives from England crammed the waiting areas, and Chester found himself desperately searching the sea of faces for Roberta, unaware that a massive hunt for her had already been undertaken. Disappointed, he gripped his luggage and started toward the taxi stands and the overzealous drivers vying for his fare. He had gone only a few feet when a dark young man approached him. Chester, assuming that this was one of the drivers, handed over his suitcase. But something in the tilt of the young man's chin and the curve of his brow made him pause.

"Are you Chester?" Slim asked.

"Yes, I'm Chester Daley," he replied a little too quickly. "Where's Roberta?"

"I'm her brother, Slim... Roberta's been missing since last night."

Chester was soon surrounded by Roberta's brothers and sisters who had come to receive him. Caleb, having borrowed a car from a friend, made the long, weary journey back to the little cottage. The spectacular sweep of landscape was lost on Chester, and he hardly heard the mocking laughter of the sea as it crashed against the jagged rocks. Later, all he was to remember of that journey was the end of it, with Hannah standing tall in the doorway of the cottage, arms held wide. To Chester, her cascading hair and high cheekbones suggested a beautiful dark goddess. She looked stronger than he had expected, but when he gathered her in his arms, he felt her quiver like a broken butterfly.

Roberta's fluffy slippers lay where she had left them, and Chester, recognizing them, blinked back mist from his eyes. He found the little room prepared for him pleasant and, full of unexpected exhaustion, threw himself down on the clean sheets.

Later in the afternoon when he awoke, he stared at the ceiling, not daring to move or even to breathe, hoping that during his rest things had been sorted out and all was well with Roberta. But the house was too still, too expectant. A sudden commotion brought him to his feet. It was Caleb, breathless and wild-eyed. "Mama! Everybody! Come quick!"

The house almost shook out of its foundations from the scampering feet. But Caleb only paused momentarily in the little kitchen before heading out again. "Come down to the beach!" he screamed.

As Chester made his way with the others down the rocky cliff path, the sight of a fishing boat on the shore sent a shiver through him, and his last remaining hope died in his throat. Even before he got there, he could see flame-coloured hair matted with seaweed hanging over the bough, and knew that the body covered by the sailcloth was Roberta's.

Hannah collapsed in the sand, years of wringing hands over Roberta finally culminating in tragedy. The children were struck down one by one, carrying their grief like sirens on the wind. When Chester eventually saw Roberta's face, she looked like a pale water nymph. And when he dared to touch her cheeks, he found them unbearably cold. So cold that he crumpled into the sand, his heart breaking right on the beach. After that he remembered the warm hands of Roberta's sisters leading him back to the cottage where Hannah, the goddess, held them all fiercely in a bond of love.

Chester's short stay extended to six weeks. He moved his things into the little living room under protest from Hannah, but she finally gave in when he wouldn't have it any other way. Everyone in the household drew strength from his presence.

During the long days, he remained close to the house, helping out with chores and seeing to minor repairs. But in the hot evenings he became a solitary figure wandering along the rocky cliff path, forever staring out to sea, as though answering the call of the lonely swallows who hid among the cruel rocks. Sad hazel eyes watched his every move, silently willing him back to safety, but when, on the wildest days, he meandered aimlessly along the treacherous cliffs, unmindful of danger, the sure-footed Georgina would always be sent to lead him back home safely.

The family found that by the time he was to return to England they had developed a bond with him and would surely miss him. After his departure, a London solicitor contacted them with news about their windfall. Roberta's entire inheritance from her aunt would be equally divided among her brothers and sisters. And Hannah was shocked to learn of her own inheritance.

It wasn't until three years after Roberta's death that Chester Daley returned to the island. He had found it impossible to shake off the memories of the time he had spent with the Douglases. Many times in London he would suddenly feel a twinge of something in the air, hear a certain sound, or perhaps even feel the wind blow just so, and he would be transported back to the Jamaican cliffs, with the wind at his back, and feel a pair of soft, loving hands lead him on and on. There was no denying the urgency. He had to see it, feel it, all again.

He didn't inform anyone about his arrival, didn't search out anyone in the waiting crowd. Filled with unexpected buoyancy, he welcomed the squabbles of the higglers and taxi drivers, and a rush of memories flew along with him in the cab as the salt on the wind exhilarated him and the spectacular cliffs, palms, hibiscuses, and roaring sea all seemed to greet him.

When the cab pulled up to the Douglases' property, the run-down little cottage was gone. In its place stood a large modern home surrounded by a well-tended garden. Chester's heart leaped into his throat. They must have moved, he thought, and was about to ask the driver to turn around when he made out, under the aquamarine sky, the figure of a young woman tending the plants. Quickly paying his fare, Chester added a hefty tip and, with suitcase in hand, hurried headlong from the cab as though driven by something intangible and irresistible.

Approaching the young woman, he was struck by her fierce, dark beauty. It was Georgina. Sunlight danced in her long curly black hair, and when her large, surprised hazel eyes met his, Chester knew what had brought him back to this tropical family. He smiled as dimples stood out in Georgina's cheeks, and she held out her slim arms in welcome.

I, Caleb Douglas, had always wanted to be an artist, but my dreams were secretive and private. I longed to create, though cheap lead pencils were my only tools, and I hoarded discarded brown wrapping paper, clean backs of old greeting cards, and leftover ruled sheets from exercise books to use for my sketches.

My free moments were spent sketching, and this solitary pastime might well have gone on indefinitely had it not been that on reaching eighteen I accepted a paying position as kitchen help in one of the Montego Bay hotels. With my older brother, Slim, already working there, I knew the job would be menial, but in our circumstances three pounds per week was inviting.

Most days it wasn't until late in the evenings before Slim and I could hurry home, anxious as roosting birds and so worn out that immediately after our meagre suppers we would fall asleep while the rest of the family engaged in conversation.

During lunch hour, I often wandered away from the hotel compound. One such afternoon, feeling particularly restless, I followed the meandering shoreline of the hotel's beachfront. I ignored fences and barriers and strayed into adjoining properties until I came upon a rustic strip of sand known locally as Pelican Beach. The shoreline was dark and muddy, supporting the growth of wild mangrove trees and straggly coconut palms. I saw driftwood, hotel refuse, and the skeletons of abandoned boats and paddles scattered in the surf, and I felt as abandoned as the litter blowing along that hot beach. Lonely, I imagined myself a solitary figure in the wind, when a sound, like that of the cracking of a whip, startled me. A sudden flight of swallows and seagulls beat the air with their strong wings. I knew I must have disturbed them, or someone else was on the beach. Instinctively I turned and saw that an artist was setting up her equipment beneath the mangrove overhang.

I approached cautiously. Something other than my usual timid self prompted me. The artist was so intent in her work that she wasn't aware of me until I was almost level with her. She was fair-skinned and wore a wide-brimmed straw hat to protect herself against the sun, and a white Sea Island cotton shirt that billowed in the breeze over her cutoff denim shorts. Her legs were long and shapely, and her freckled arms looked strong. Her brushstrokes were sure, and around her wrist I glimpsed a strand of purplish Job's tears seeds. Why would she wear such a bracelet, I wondered, since all of us locals were reluctant to wear them, feeling they would bring bad luck? I concluded that she was foreign.

"Hello there," she said, looking up. "You gave me a shock!"

From her speech I could tell she was Jamaican like myself and not a tourist. "I'm sorry," I said shyly. "I shouldn't have come over." My words were stilted and formal. She smiled and stood away from the canvas, affording me a better look at her work. I didn't say anything; words were stuck like plum seeds in my throat.

"So what do you think?" she asked confidently, nodding at the painting.

What did I think? Oh, I wish I could have told her. The painting was extraordinary. In fact, her eye for detail was uncanny. She hadn't missed the browning palms, the choppy sea, the boats, or the conch shells.

"It's good," I said, finally managing to speak. "It's quite good."

She threw back her head and laughed heartily, and I had a rare opportunity to really look at her. She seemed about twenty-five, her complexion was flawless, and her eyes were pale grey.

"You wouldn't just say that, would you?" she asked, bursting into my thoughts.

"No, I mean it. It's really good." I searched her oval face for something that might miraculously prolong our chance conversation.

She laughed. "Well, it's not really my work. It belongs to a student who's about to graduate. I'm just the chaperone for the girls from Kingston Art School."

"Well, it's brilliant, anyway. But if you're the chaperone, as you say, why are you out here alone?"

"The students have gone farther down the beach for a break. I was just helping to spread some glazes for this student, you know, to help bring out the colours."

"You shouldn't stay out here alone. Know what I mean?"

"I know what you mean, but so what? Artists should be able to work anywhere without being disturbed by nosy people like you!"

"Well, excuse me," I said, instinctively stepping aside. "You're wrong about me. But as for you, how come a smart, good-looking woman like you doesn't know the first thing about being careful on an isolated beach? You don't think you'd attract men?" I turned away, heart pounding, before she had a chance to respond.

"Wait!" she called out after me. "I was rude. I apologize." She held out her hand.

It was a slim, pale hand that seemed to reach across years, for when I looked at her more closely, it occurred to me that perhaps she was older than I had first thought. There was even a possibility that she could be over forty! I wasn't sure what to make of her, but when she reached out so tentatively, her fingers touched my hand and I knew I had to forgive her.

"It's all right," I said, turning away again. "But I better get back to work."

"Please wait," she insisted. "My name's Valerie Ingram. What's yours?"

I stopped. There was such a presence about her. It was almost as though she were the wild sea itself. I felt myself drifting, drowning, fighting against her tide, until at last I lay frozen in the warmth of her half smile.

"My name's Caleb Douglas."

"Come here often?"

"Not really. What about you?"

"Sort of." She laughed, covering her mouth with her free hand. "I usually come here with students from the school in Kingston every second month or so."

I hardly heard what she said and was surprised to hear myself speaking my thoughts out loud. "Why do you wear Job's tears? Don't you know they bring nothing but bad luck and only tourists can get away with wearing them?"

She snorted. "Nonsense! Don't tell me you believe in that backward mumbo jumbo."

"Yes, I do. Mark my words, those things bring tears."

"What about John crow beads? Do they bring John crows?"

"Don't make fun of it," I warned, walking away and feeling foolish as her cool eyes stung my back. I was glad she couldn't see my face, glad I couldn't see hers, since she must have guessed at my poverty and poor education. I supposed that as far as she was concerned, I must be totally backward. And I wanted nothing more than to prove myself to her.

"By the way, do you paint?" she called out after me.

"No!" I called back sharply, then softened. "I draw. I'm always drawing."

"You what?" she shouted, deafened by the roar of the sea.

"I said I draw!"

"I'd like to see your work," she said, leaning into the wind.

"I have to go," I protested. "I work over at the Sea Horse

Hotel in the kitchen, and I'm late already."

"Well, how about bringing some sketches with you tomorrow, same time, same place?"

I was suddenly nervous, full of the fear of criticism, exposure, and rejection. What if she told me I was only wasting my time. I held my head down in anguish, unable to meet her eyes, but the wind spoke my reply. "Yes! Yes! Yes!" it cried.

"Tomorrow," I replied. Then, remembering my lack of training, I turned self-consciously to face her. "Nobody's ever looked at my drawings. I never had any instruction, so you might not like them." I waited for her reply with a pounding heart and hoped that its loud beating wouldn't expose me for the idiot that I was.

Then I watched in a trance as she put the varnish brush and her hat aside. I saw her auburn hair float like a sail on the breeze as she cupped her hands and called above the sea's roar. "That's even better, because it means you're an original."

And I didn't know whether to laugh or cry.

That evening at home my thoughts were in confusion, one moment hopeful, the next full of dread. I searched out my drawings one by one, retrieving each from its hiding place: under a floorboard or a mattress, in a drawer under clothes. Then I rolled each piece into a cardboard tube, careful to choose only those that excited my senses. Black strands of my hair fell across my eyes, and I prayed that I would be calm and not let myself down.

The next morning I rose early as usual. I was aware of a certain stillness except for the occasional clink of a teacup against a saucer. And I knew that although the rest of the household might still be asleep, Papa was up and having his cocoa. I held back momentarily, too wracked with insecurity to emerge from my room. When I finally crossed the threshold, Papa's eyes met mine across the kitchen table where the hot pepper pickle jar, Pick a Pepper sauce, guava jelly, Andrew's Liver Salts, and Milo tin crowded one another on bamboo mats.

In middle age Papa's face had settled into a handsome cast, only a whisper of grey invading his thick, dark hair. He looked tired, almost resigned, but one glance from him pinned me to my chair, and my grip automatically tightened around my cardboard tube of drawings.

"Morning, Caleb," he said, smiling, his blue-veined hands lying solidly on his place mat, his dusky countenance brightened by the unusual green of his eyes.

"Morning, Papa," I said. "Morning, Mama," I added, suddenly noticing her by the stove.

She glanced sideways at me. "Morning, Caleb." Smiling, she quickly poured out another cup of the steaming liquid. "Here," she said, coming over to the table, "have a cup before you go to work."

"Thanks, Mama. Where's Slim?" I asked, hoping the question would act as a diversion and shift the focus from me and, ultimately, off my drawings.

"Slim going stop off at the post office before him go into work," Mama said, continuing to heat the cocoa. "Miss James, the postmistress, say we get mail, so somebody must come pick it up."

"I just hope it's not some bad news," Papa said, bending low over his second cup.

Mama's eyes narrowed, a smile hidden in her cheeks. "George, don't you go setting your mouth on things. You Scottish people have 'goat mouth,' and we know that mean you can make things happen that wouldn't normally happen, so just you be still."

Papa responded with a wink and a good-natured click of his teeth. He might have laughed, too, had two of my sisters not come bouncing into the room.

"Mama, Mama!" the youngest one, Maggie, wailed. "Elaine took away my hair clasps and I wanted to wear them to school, and now she making monkey faces after me."

"Calm down, you two," Mama scolded. "Whatever happened to 'Good morning'?"

"Good morning!" both girls chimed, coming over to sit with us.

Elaine sighed heavily, then smiled coyly. And I wondered if Papa would be taken in. She moved closer, her hair cascading around her face.

"Look, Papa," she coaxed, "my hair's a mess. It's thick and ugly and full of tangles. Can I cut it?"

Papa's neck muscles stiffened as he glared at her. "You can forget about cutting your hair. I like my daughters to look like girls, not plucked chickens." There was a hint of a smile in his cheeks as Mama chuckled over by the stove. And when I turned away and caught Maggie's eye, she, too, was smiling. But Elaine wasn't finished yet.

"Please, Papa," she pleaded.

But Papa just leaned heavily on his elbows and lifted a finger to his lips. "Sssh! Never start a day off with an argument. It bound to spoil the rest of your day. And another thing, tie back your hair. Go get a piece of ribbon from Mama. It will help tame your lovely hair if anything can."

Elaine did her best to conceal the smile that slowly spread across her face as she basked in the light of the indirect compliment. Then, turning to Mama, she sounded almost triumphant. "So can I have some pieces of ribbon?"

"The first thing you do is plait your hair," Mama said. "You're right about one thing. Your hair's thick, but it's very pretty. A long braid down your back will suit you to a T."

Maggie had sat quietly throughout the whole exchange, but as I glanced over at her, I could tell she had quickly lost interest in the turn of events. "Where's everybody else?" she asked, addressing no one in particular.

Mama looked up from the cocoa. "Sheila and Slim had to leave early, so you better go wake the others. Tell them the cocoa's ready."

"Do I have to?" Maggie whined, but one glance from Papa set her on her feet.

I gulped down my cocoa, grabbed my drawings, and went to wash up quickly, then headed to work. By the time I got there, the cook was already on duty and putting the finishing touches to breakfast. I put my drawings away in one of the supply cupboards and settled into my tasks. I knew that Slim made it in on time, as well, because I saw him walk past the kitchen, but there was no opportunity to speak with him, so I kept the pent-up excitement about my appointment with Valerie Ingram to myself.

By the time afternoon came, I was impatient to leave. I didn't have to return to work until two o'clock. Therefore, I would have enough time to get to Pelican Beach and back. I followed the same route as the day before, only this time my impatience was apparent as I raced headlong across the sand. High in the blue sky, I noticed a flock of John crows circling. The air was putrid, filled with the stench of a dead animal, and I wanted nothing more than to be out of the downwind.

As I drew closer, I saw Valerie in the company of some young artists. They were sitting astride wooden donkeys, sketching. I was terribly disappointed. I had hoped she would be alone. Then she saw me and came over immediately.

"Caleb, did you bring your drawings?"

I told her I had and waved the cardboard tube at her, delighting in the pleasure I saw in her eyes.

"Good. Let's get away from here." She glanced briefly at her companions before we headed down the beach and stopped under the shelter of a spreading mangrove.

"These are just a few of my pieces," I said nervously, my throat dry and tight. Valerie carefully extracted the roll of drawings from the tube. My heart refused to beat, and I searched her face for any expression that might disclose her thoughts. Digging my toes into the sand, I was afraid of revealing the trembling that gripped me. When Valerie glanced up, I wasn't sure what to think. Nothing betrayed her thoughts.

"You have a gift," she said throatily. "I wonder if you realize you have a natural understanding of perspective. Your lines are beautifully uncluttered."

"What you mean by that?" I blurted, regretting my words the moment I said them.

She laughed, as I knew she would. "It means you're darn good!"

I was stunned. I honestly hadn't expected praise, and I sat there like a slack-mouthed idiot.

"Mind you," she continued, "I'm not a teacher, but I've been around enough art and artists to know good stuff. I'm a patron of the art school. Basically, what that boils down to, is that besides being on the board of directors and acting as chaperone to the students, I also have a say in major decisions, you know, stuff like who gets admitted, who can get scholarships, and such. Have you ever thought about applying?"

I shook my head absently, too embarrassed to meet her direct gaze.

She leaned closer and smiled. "Why don't I think before I say things? It's the money, isn't it? Would a scholarship offer change your mind?"

"I couldn't," I replied, managing to ease the words out of my parched throat. "My family...we're poor."

There was no need to say anything else. Being Jamaican herself, Valerie was no stranger to how tough economic times affected families such as mine. She bit her lip as though attempting to swallow words that might get in the way, then grabbed me by the shoulders, her face aglow with renewed excitement.

"Listen, you should paint. I'd really like to see what you could do with colour. I can supply you with proper sketch pads and a set of watercolours and brushes."

"Why?" I asked suspiciously.

She didn't answer right away. She sensed my pride, sensed protest rising in my throat and, armed with only a smile, managed to cut off any further opposition on my part. "It's really nothing more than my way of thanking you for sharing your work with me. And you know what? I have a whole lot of art supplies here. I won't be coming back to Montego Bay for a couple of months, so until such time, you could show me whatever you manage to come up with. You owe it to yourself to be the best you can be."

After she put it like that, I couldn't help but share her infectious laughter.

That night as Slim and I walked home from work I was tempted to tell him about what had happened. But he was too excited about local news he had overheard discussed at the tables: sugarcane farmworkers were on strike in the Eastern Parishes, and the Farmworkers Union was trying to get them back out to work; the bauxite industry was really taking off near Mandeville; and the price of sugarcane had gone up in Europe. I barely commented on the situations because I was too caught up with observing how beautifully the breadfruit, poinciana, and tamarind trees were silhouetted against the night sky. All I could think about was taking out my recently acquired bundle of art supplies, so I could begin painting in earnest.

The evening, in spite of its normalcy, concealed something ominous in the air. The feeling was nagging me when Slim suddenly halted.

"Look," he said, "all the lights are off at home. That's unusual." His words hung like icicles in the cool night air. Following his gaze, I saw the cottage in darkness. Were it not for a flickering glow in the front room, the cottage would have been invisible. It was blanketed by crouching darkness, imperceptibly pressed against the black rock face that jutted into the sea.

"Poor Mama," Slim said. "She waited all day to read this letter and now it's too dark at home for her to read it."

"You're right!" I said, remembering the letter that had been discussed briefly at breakfast.

Slim pulled the envelope from his pocket and pondered it in the moonlight. He weighed the envelope in his hands, as if that would reveal its contents and satisfy our curiosity. "Wonder who it could be from. The postmark's London, England, but it doesn't have a return address. And it's definitely for Mama."

An involuntary chill ran up my spine, and I couldn't help feeling that it might have been better if that wretched letter hadn't come. Slim sensed my misgivings and smiled. It was the same way Papa had of smiling in the face of disaster.

"Hurry up," he said with a grin. "The sooner we get home, the sooner we'll know what it's about."

We raced up the path, and the resulting crunch of our shoes on the gravel alerted Mama, who met us at the front door, storm lantern in hand. "You don't know how glad I be to see you both. Don't worry. Everybody okay. We have a power failure. Your sisters gone to bed and your father step out to buy a bun. I was hoping he meet up with you two."

"It's a moonlit night," I said, trying to ease her agitation. Was she worried about the letter?

Then, as if reading my thoughts, she asked, "Slim, did you get that letter at all?"

"Yes, Mama, I have it right here."

"Thanks. Let me just serve both of you some beef soup. You must be hungry. It's so late. Then I sit down and try to read the letter by the lantern."

I will always remember the patterns of light that flickered across the kitchen's stucco walls as Slim and I sat hunched over our bowls, hardly daring to look up, our eyes peeled for crawling insects and flying bugs. Mama sat at the head of the table, her face illuminated by the lantern's glow. For a long time it seemed as if she were holding her breath. Except for the occasional click of our spoons against our bowls, silence reigned.

"But wait," Slim said, "you're not going to open the letter?"

The silence was broken, and I glanced up quickly, noticing that Mama had already opened the envelope. Her sure fingers caressed the folded sheets of blue paper, and I watched as she slowly straightened each page. Something of my anticipation brought to mind my recent encounter with Valerie, and I reached down beside me and felt my little bundle of art supplies, experiencing a rush of pleasure that they were real. The joy of my pounding heart drowned out all sound, and I could have sworn Mama's voice was coming from a long way off. Had I fallen asleep? I looked up, suddenly jolted back to consciousness as I realized she was talking about the letter.

"You won't believe this," she said. "It be from my older sister, Melanie."

"Is that so?" Slim said, craning his neck toward the letter.

"Yes," Mama said. "She live in England for years, though she never keep in touch. She run a grocery store in London, and it looks like she do well. Because here it is. She offer to send for one of you children to go to England to study. Imagine, a chance to study over there. Everything paid for and a place to stay. Well, how about it, Slim?"

Slim's spoon fell with a clatter. He quickly pulled his chair away from the table, the wood screaming against the smooth floor. Suddenly the golden glow of the lantern was no longer comfortable.

"Not me, Mama," Slim said, shaking his head in desperation. "I'm settled in my job at the hotel, and who knows, I might even get a promotion."

Mama turned to me. "What about you, Caleb? Your Aunt Melanie say nursing is booming in England, and it's for both men and women. Think about it, Caleb. Hospital workers always in demand. And another thing, the money be not bad."

"Oh, Mama," I said quickly, "you're forgetting that I didn't even finish high school. No school in England would take me without a Senior Cambridge or a GCE certificate. I'm better off holding on to my job here. And remember, Mama, Papa needs all the help he can get. And I'm willing to help."

Mama sighed knowingly. I was right. The family couldn't survive on just Papa's salary. Although I couldn't see Mama's hands after she let them fall into her lap, I knew she was clenching and unclenching her fingers the way she always did.

"So I guess is going to be Roberta," she said finally. "She the oldest girl. She going to be eighteen soon and she graduating high school next month. It has to be her. But don't say nothing. Let me talk to your father first."

During the next few days, I pushed the consequences of the letter into the back of my mind. I became absorbed in my water-colours and eagerly experimented with different techniques. However, my first attempts were tentative, hesitant, and raw, occasionally even unsuccessful. Sometimes I could be found pressed against our rattling windowpanes, privy to the command-ing view of blue that would soon be reflected in my wild painted skies and horizons full of interacting oranges, blues, and greens and the sporadic splash of deep purple. I found it necessary to duplicate the exact shade of red of the wild hibiscuses that dotted the terrain. Blue-black John crows swooped and circled in the periphery of my paintings, and a viewer's eye would be unconsciously directed away from our humble cottage to the magnificence of the headland.

I longed to paint people, longed to capture the untamed beauty of my sister, Roberta; the serenity of my mother; and the gentleness of my father and brother. But unfortunately shyness held me back. In the end, it was only because Roberta was so enigmatic that she unknowingly invaded my creative expression. It happened when I was sent on an errand to Cornwall Beach to deliver packaged lunches for the cook.

No one was more surprised than I to see Roberta on the beach, looking comfortable and animated in the company of a group of tourists. I was grateful she didn't see me, because I saw a certain look on her face, a look of rapture that transcended the moment and seemed to crackle in the flash of her reddish hair and the glint of her green eyes. "Roberta, Roberta," I whispered under my breath. "Roberta, I love you." But I stopped myself from calling out, realizing she wouldn't welcome my intrusion. I respected her privacy by keeping out of her way, allowing her to be herself. But the memory of her sitting there so relaxed in the company of strangers etched itself indelibly in my subconscious and poured itself out from the tips of my paintbrushes into an unforgettable painting I timidly titled *Roberta on the Beach*.

Watercolours consumed me, and I was amazed at how quickly the pages of my sketch pads were filled.

One morning, arriving at work, I sensed excitement in the air and was informed by Alfred, the cook, that a white woman had come to see me the previous evening. When she couldn't find me, she left a note. I tore the message open the moment I got time to myself. A dim bulb hanging from the end of a long electrical cord was my only source of light as my eyes flew over the hastily written note.

Dear Caleb:

Just a note to let you know I'll be coming to MoBay with some students on June 25. It's a little sooner than we would normally be coming back, but I'm anxious to see your watercolours. Meet me at Pelican Beach on Friday at lunchtime, and don't forget the paintings.

Cordially, Valerie

How I wished I had had more time. What would Valerie think of the paintings I had done so far? Friday, as far as I was concerned, might as well have been the day of judgement.

On Friday afternoon I dragged my heels as I crossed the sand, heading for Pelican Beach, sketch pad in hand.

"Hi, Caleb!" Valerie shouted, seeing me approach. "Good. You brought the watercolours." She didn't waste a moment on small talk. Right there, out in the direct sunlight, she lifted the cover of one of my sketch pads.

"Some of those pieces are just tryouts," I said nervously, but she didn't respond.

It was as though she were beyond hearing. Her eyes darted over the pages, and her index finger ran over the textures.

"These are so good. You know, you could sell these in Kingston."

I didn't know what to say, then remembered the painting *Roberta on the Beach.* "Not the one with the girl on the beach, though."

"Why not? That's one of your better ones."

"Because," I said, lowering my voice, "it's my sister. I couldn't sell her."

"All right then, but what sort of prices should we be asking?"

"I have no idea. Why don't you decide? You know more about these things."

"Well, for starters, I'm going to buy this one of the cottage on the hill. I think it's worth about eight pounds."

That was how my business association with Valerie Ingram began, and thanks to it, our modest celebration on Roberta's birthday, combined with her high-school graduation, was a success.

Looking back now, I sometimes regret that neither Slim nor I had been as brave as Roberta and taken up the gauntlet. I can't help but feel that Roberta's chance at a future was our chance untaken. Even when she boarded the plane, looking so proud and confident, our timid hearts flew along with her. But mine was already broken when the final metallic scream of the engines filled my ears and struck me down.

A year later our beloved father died unexpectedly. His heart could no longer hold out. I wondered if he missed Roberta as much as I did. Slim and I managed to keep the family going, and kept the girls in school, including Roberta, since it was at our insistence that she didn't come home to say a final farewell to Papa. But Roberta left us stranded; her letters became few and far between.

How quickly the years raced by. Before long I was practically living off my art sales. Slim was now the headwaiter at the hotel, and

Georgina was out of high school. Roberta had been away for a long time. Sometimes when I looked at my mother's face I shuddered. She had become too pale, too drawn, and streaks of grey had invaded her hair. I wondered if she was pining for Papa, and Roberta.

When Roberta finally did come home, it felt as if she had never left. Unfortunately she got on everyone's nerves. Lorraine felt she was a stranger. Sheila was tired of her disapproval. And Roberta's acquired English accent grated on everyone.

All of us felt Roberta suspected that Chester Daley, her Scottish boyfriend, wouldn't fit in with our poverty, so she worked hard at trying to force us to fit in with him. "It's a sign of nervousness," Slim said.

Why wasn't I more sensitive to Roberta's turmoil? Maybe then I could have prevented her disappearance. She wasn't in the house on the morning of Chester's arrival. A set of lone footprints leading from the house to the beach were the only clues. Where did she go during the night? Why weren't we more vigilant?

It was fortunate that Valerie was in Montego Bay. She was staying at the Coral Reef Hotel in room 403. I knew that number well. It was where we transacted business, and where I was paid for my art sales, art that now hung in the Contemporary Artists Art Gallery in Kingston. On impulse I decided to ask Valerie for a favour.

Her hotel was more luxurious than the one where Slim and I worked. Crossing the large red-tiled lobby nervously, I made my way up the deep-piled stairs, breaking into a sweat. I barely knocked twice on her door before it opened. It was Valerie.

"Can I borrow your car?" I asked frantically.

"What's the matter, Caleb?" she asked, her forehead creased by a frown. "You look as if you've had a shock."

"You're right. Everything's going wrong. My sister disappeared, the one from England. And her boyfriend is coming from England today. We're supposed to pick him up at the airport."

"What do you mean your sister disappeared? People don't disappear in MoBay! You sure she's not visiting someone?"

"You don't know the half of it," I said. "She was only wearing her nightie. Mama is desperate, and my brother and sisters have organized a search party. But all I could think of is that the car might help."

"God, Caleb, this sounds serious. Only her nightgown, you say? I hope she's all right. She's the pretty one in that painting, isn't she? Caleb, take the car for the day. Don't worry. It has enough gas."

"God bless you," I said quickly, hugging her. "I'll take care of the car."

Valerie drew closer and put her arms around my shivering body, holding me so close that I let my head sink into the crook of her shoulder, where I breathed in the fragrance of fresh-cut flowers and sunlight. Tears crept stealthily down my cheeks, and she kissed them away with quiet reassurances. Then, growing more urgent, we melted gratefully into each other's eager caresses. With my face buried in the scent of her hair, I momentarily forgot my tribulation.

Hot as the flame of a candle, Valerie explored my shivering flesh, her hands as eager as my own in their groping. Quick as the blade of a cutlass, we tore at each other's clothes. I was amazed at how she matched my mounting ardour. She had the surety of a mare challenging a race against years, against the strict Jamaican class system, against the different colours of our skin, even against the unique danger of my immediate family concerns. Thinking all this, I gave in to my desire completely, and Valerie met my every thrust.

Long afterward we lay in each other's arms like survivors of a battle. How perfect the world felt at that moment. I loved this woman, I told myself, and the thought took me by surprise. Although I wanted to, I was too timid to voice my feelings. I was a weary traveller returning from a glorious, unexpected heaven, and I wondered if there was any possibility that sensible Valerie echoed my ecstasy. Then, suddenly, I remembered Roberta, and guilt crashed into my thoughts.

Valerie must have sensed my turmoil, for pale as a water lily, she placed a finger to lips so recently sweetened with our kisses. For the longest time she held me in a loving gaze, a look that spoke of laughter yet to come, gratification, and hope. "Caleb, I'm over forty. Forty-two to be exact."

I sighed. "It doesn't matter." Then, with great reluctance, I gave her a parting kiss that lingered on my lips for some time after. "I really must go. We mustn't forget my sister."

She squeezed my hand and, with downcast eyes, let me go. "Hurry! Take the car and God be with you."

Neither of us said another word about what had just happened, but as I walked away I knew her eyes were still on me.

When I returned to our humble house, Slim asked suspiciously, "Where'd you get the car?"

"A friend from Kingston lent it to me for the day."

"Is it that white woman I've been hearing about?"

"Yes… We can use her station wagon to pick up Chester and look for Roberta, too."

"I don't think we're going to find her," he said.

I noticed a look in his eye, a sharp sadness, an expression as brittle as coal. Slim sensed I knew that neither of us believed Roberta would be found alive.

There's been no word," he whispered.

I nodded. "I know. I can tell."

Later our excited sisters cleaned the station wagon so there was room among Valerie's art supplies for all of us. And when we all crammed excitedly into the vehicle, our only regret was that Mama would be left behind. But it was what she wanted. "Just in case she returns," she said hopefully.

Chester wasn't anything like I had imagined. Maybe it was because I had a tendency to think all Scottish men were like my Grandpa Trevor: dark-haired and ruddy. On the contrary, Chester was fair with pale blue eyes. And he had a trim, athletic build, unlike Grandpa, who had been stocky.

"Where's Roberta?" were the first words I heard him utter, and I liked the way he said her name. There was no hiding the affection, and I wanted to protect him from the hurt to come. When he wrinkled his brow, I saw his eyes dart to each of our faces. We all wanted to reassure him that everything was well, but we couldn't.

On the way home I noticed that his eyes had become unfocused and took no delight in the crashing of the waves against the rocks, or the funny little donkeys carrying produce, or even the boisterous higglers in bright prints selling fruit along the roadside. Mama liked Chester immediately, and I knew the feeling was mutual. I could tell by the wan smiles on both of their faces—expressions of hope, of joy, of sadness and sorrow. And when Chester fell into a sudden, fitful sleep, Mama called us together.

"Come, Sheila, Lorraine, Elaine, Maggie, Georgina, and you, too, Caleb and Slim. Let us join hands and ask God and the spirit of your father to protect your sister wherever she is. And another thing, this man Chester seem like a good man, and we ask the Lord to spare him from pain."

And there, pressed against our windowpanes, I glimpsed the wide expanse of sea and felt the presence of Roberta. Slowly I let my hands fall free of the loving circle and heard her say as if she were in the room, "Come, Caleb, come down to the beach." As I slipped out the door, I didn't say a word to the others.

No wind ruffled the heads of the wild hibiscuses or dry bracken. All was strangely quiet. My eyes wandered as far as the horizon, and then I saw it: a fishing boat as white as snow, just a little larger than a speck. I squinted into the sun and saw a flash of red, then a line of white spray and foam in the wake of the boat. It was then that I knew for certain. Roberta was truly gone. I raced with breakneck speed up the hillside to the cottage and burst into the kitchen like a wild, wounded animal whose cries could easily be heard for miles.

"Mama! Everybody! Come quick! Come down to the beach!" The wooden floors rattled menacingly under my feet as I ran out again under the clear, cloudless sky. My heart was heavy and black with rage that stung at my eyes with streaming tears.

Chester, Mama, and the others tore after me down the path to the sea where a piece of my heart was irrevocably wrenched from me. There, on the beach, we saw an old fisherman. He was crusty and black, with great sad eyes and a voice as soft as the foam that still clung to his boat. "Good day," he said. At that exact moment we all knew Roberta's fate.

❦

Mama was our consolation, our confidante, our source of strength. When Chester decided to extend his stay, he took us by surprise, though we were more than grateful for his company. His presence was a comfort to us. I don't know how often I would sit and watch him doing trivial or tedious tasks and think that he was the man Roberta had loved. He was like a brother to me, and whenever he wandered off along the treacherous cliffs, my heart stood still. Only Georgina had the courage to go after him. There wasn't a task that escaped his willing hands, and not a head among ours too heavy for his strong shoulders to support.

When Chester left us, it was an unnaturally cold day. The sea was wild and menacing as though a storm were brewing. Waves lashed the shore in a great show of strength, and the skies took on the deep purple hue of my paintings. Fittingly, all our hearts were grey with equal sorrow.

A month later we learned of our inheritance. Aunt Melanie left the bulk of her estate to Mama and Roberta, but now Roberta's share was to be divided among her brothers and sisters. We had been through so much together that I felt this was the perfect time to tell my family about the joy of my art, and about Valerie.

When I told her about my painting, Mama smiled. "Caleb, you don't think I suspect all along? Who you think do the dusting?

Who you think clean the house? I just waiting for you to say something." She stared at me for a long time, then shook her head. "What about the white woman I been hearing about? You don't know news travel fast in small towns?"

I sighed. "Mama, that's Valerie Ingram. She's the one who's helped me all these years. She's the one who sells my work in Kingston and gets it into shows."

"Caleb, you in love with her?"

"She's a good woman...I don't know."

"I thought I hear she older than you. You lovers?"

"Yes, Mama, but only recently. She's in her forties, but it doesn't matter.

"Caleb, Caleb, who am I to judge? If you love her, what does it matter?"

"Maybe I do love her. I can't imagine life without her."

A day or so after our conversation a letter arrived from England for Mama. The sender was Dr. Suleika Ramsaroop, and Mama was just as curious as we were to find out what it was all about.

"Who is this doctor?" Georgina and Lorraine asked, each slipping an arm around Mama's waist.

"Is it bad news?" Elaine asked, sounding every inch like Papa.

"Is from a friend of Roberta's in England," Mama finally said. "They go to school together there. She only just learn your sister pass away. She extend condolences, say she fond of Roberta and want to come see us in Jamaica."

"When will she be coming?" Lorraine asked eagerly.

"Well, is up to us," Mama said. "I wonder what she think of us all."

"Oh, God," Lorraine gasped, "so we're going to have foreign company again!"

"Too bad it's not Chester coming back," Georgina added from behind the veil of her long black hair.

"Chester was like family," Sheila said. "This will be different."

"Well, the first thing different is we never hear of this Dr. Ramsaroop before," Mama said thoughtfully. "Of course, Roberta never write much to us about anything."

Even with this backdrop of excitement over Suleika's letter, I experienced a strange loneliness. The reason was obvious: I missed Valerie. It had been months since I had last seen her. Too consumed with grief over Roberta, it only now occurred to me that I hadn't laid eyes on Valerie since I returned her car on that fateful day. She had promised to come back soon, but she hadn't, and I had hardly noticed. Now I wondered if she had left a message for me at the hotel where she usually stayed.

When I checked, there was a letter and, according to the date scribbled in the corner, it had sat there for months. Out in the bright sunshine I eagerly ripped open the envelope, and a thin, pale note fluttered into my hand.

Dear Caleb:

I won't be in Montego Bay for quite some time. Don't be surprised. I've been asked to accompany a group of students over to Denmark. They'll be attending an art school there called Kuntz for six months. Sorry I didn't have a chance to tell you this in person, but since I still don't know your address, I took a chance and left this note here for you at the hotel. Your paintings are in high demand at the gallery in Kingston, so if you feel like sending a few more of your pieces, a friend of mine, a curator, is usually in Montego Bay on Fridays. He likes the privacy of Pelican Beach, so quite often he can be found there. His name is Purnell Barnes. Anyway, take care until I see you—Valerie.

So she was in Europe, I thought. How I wished I had spoken to her before she had left. That Friday, on a sudden whim, I decided to go to Pelican Beach. The place was exactly the way I had last seen it, except for a group of gangly young men frolicking in the sea.

I wandered over and asked, "Is one of you Purnell Barnes?"

"I'm Purnell," a tall, wide-eyed brown-skinned fellow replied, peering at me suspiciously before wading onto shore. "Who wants to know?"

"I'm Caleb Douglas, Valerie Ingram's friend."

"You are!" Purnell exclaimed. "I sort of expected you to look different."

"What do you mean?" I asked sharply.

"Don't get me wrong, but from Valerie's description, I thought you'd be more destitute-looking."

"Why's that?"

"Don't take it personally, man, but the tumbledown cottage in most of your seascapes is rumoured to be your home."

"Is that so?" I snapped, disliking Barnes's attitude. "Well, I'll tell you something. I wouldn't go as far as saying we're destitute, but that little tumbledown cottage, as you call it, is home to me and my family, and a better home would be hard to find." Purnell lowered his eyes self-consciously as I continued, and I noticed a tic in his jaw. "When's Valerie coming back, anyway?" I demanded.

"What do you mean, 'coming back'?" he asked, puzzled. "You mean to MoBay?"

"No, I mean coming back to the island."

"Don't you know? She's here."

"What about Kuntz in Denmark and the students?"

"That was ages ago. Donkey's years, in fact." He stopped himself, as if he had already given me too much information. "It's just that she hasn't been too well lately," he added sheepishly.

"Not well?"

"Well, she's too sick to travel. Anyway, you know how it is."

"What the hell are you talking about?" I barked, sounding more aggressive than I ever thought I could.

"Look, man," he shouted back, "what's all this third degree? Don't you know the woman's pregnant? So there! Now you have it!"

"Oh, God!" I gasped. "How? When did this happen? When is she due?"

"For all I know she's probably had the baby already. I've been here on business for over a month. Call the people at the art school. They can give you more details."

Later that afternoon I asked permission to use the hotel phone and promised to cover the long-distance charges. I called the art school in Kingston and identified myself to the person who answered, and was surprised when he recognized my name.

"Caleb Douglas," he said, "what a pleasure this is. Your work is exquisite. What can I do for you?"

"I'm trying to locate Valerie Ingram."

"I have her number right here," the gentleman said. "She'll be glad to hear from you, especially since she's set aside a room at our gallery to display your work. I hope you have a pen handy. And if you come to Kingston, I'd love to meet you."

I copied the number quickly and almost immediately dialled it. The telephone rang six times before a woman's voice answered, speaking patois, and I knew it must be the household help.

"May I speak with Miss Ingram?" I asked.

There was a brief silence before the woman spoke. "Miss Ingram not 'ere, sar."

"Where can I reach her?"

"Di missis in hospital, sar," she said. "She not doing too well."

"What hospital is she in?"

"Is St. Joseph, but dem tell mi she not to 'ave no visitors or phone call ider. I'm di helper, name Esmie."

"Well, I'm her friend Caleb from Montego Bay. I'm an artist."

"Me know who you is. The missis left one letter 'ere for you, sar. She want to mail it, sar, to a 'otel in MoBay."

"Don't mail it!" I interrupted. "I'm coming to Kingston. Give me the address there."

As far as Mama and the others were concerned, I was going to Kingston to see an exhibition of my work. Elaine wanted to come, but because of exams couldn't take the time off from school. In the end it was Maggie, because she pleaded so pitifully, who was allowed to accompany me, since Mama insisted someone should represent the family. Mama made arrangements with an old school friend, Mrs. Edna Causewell of Constant Spring Road, for us to stay with her for a couple of days.

Neither Maggie nor myself had ever been on a train before, and at first the business of tickets and vigilant conductors was unnerving, but in the end we enjoyed it. The rattling train was mostly filled with higglers and other market-bound people who seemed to ignite the small carriage with their laughter and high voices amid the confusion of bulging crocus bags, live chickens, straw baskets of yams, cocoas, guineps, cucumbers, red peas, and star apples. Every jolt from the train scattered a quarter pint or so of red peas, and the live chickens squawked in protest as Maggie and I clung to our seats for dear life.

Among the other passengers, Maggie looked almost elegant and grown-up, although she was only fifteen. She was attractively dressed in a pale blue sundress. It set off her long brown hair and, with her dark complexion, made her look exotic. It struck me for the first time how much she reminded me of our proud sister, Roberta. She had the same tilt to her chin, the same half smile and merry eyes that looked as though they were enjoying a secret. I sat there in the close confines of the train, staring at her, teary-eyed. Then, without thinking, I confided to her my real reason for travelling to Kingston. It seemed as if Roberta herself were there, and I could almost hear my dead sister ask with her forced English accent, "What's troubling you, Caleb?"

Maggie listened, wide-eyed, then wrapped her thin arms around me affectionately. "Oh, Caleb" was all she said with a sigh.

As planned, Mrs. Causewell met us at the station. She was a heavyset, matronly woman with a yellowish complexion. Maggie recognized her instantly from Mama's description.

"So you're Hannah's children," she said. "Oh, my, you're both so tall and good-looking." Noticing our embarrassment, she quickly changed the subject. "Anyway, come, I have a car waiting."

Mrs. Causewell took an instant liking to Maggie. After a hot-stew lunch, Maggie spent the afternoon looking around the plazas with our hostess, while I used the time to find out where the gallery, St. Joseph's Hospital, and Forest Gardens were. The last was where Valerie's house was located. I took a cab there first and found brightly painted, flat-roofed houses nestled under brooding purple hillsides. Pushing open the low metal gate of number 19, I walked up the long concrete walkway to the veranda. The moment I got there a dog next door began to bark furiously. I knocked on the door and heard a shuffle of feet. When the door opened, I saw that it was the household helper. She was small and muscular with very dark skin and wore a freshly starched white cap and apron.

She eyed me momentarily, then finally spoke. "Good day, sar."

"Hello, I'm Caleb Douglas."

"Oh, is you Mr. Douglas. Mi glad you cum. The missis didn't make it, sar. She pass along last night. Mi 'ave di letter 'ere."

"Didn't make it?"

"She dead, sar. Mi jus' straighten up the 'ouse. People going cum soon."

I don't know what kept me on my feet. I gripped the letter fiercely, finding it almost offensive as tears streamed down my cheeks. Sitting down heavily on the veranda ledge, I tore open the envelope and read through a sea of tears.

Dearest Caleb:

If you are reading this letter, then you'll know I'm gone. I have loved you for a long time. I know it will be hard for you to understand, but the moment I found out about my pregnancy I knew I couldn't risk losing you or the baby. So I had to tell you I was away in Europe just so you wouldn't try to see me. Forgive me if I was wrong, but I feel that a young, handsome man like yourself couldn't bear to be stuck with a woman of my age. My dearest, these few months have been very difficult in more ways than one, but especially with my not being able to see you. Please don't judge my actions harshly. I did go to Denmark, but only for three weeks. Caleb, I could almost tell that you loved me, too. I could tell by the way you looked at me. But there is no excuse for my not telling you that I am diabetic and knew the pregnancy would be difficult. My doctor is hopeful, but it has sapped my strength, and I truly feel I am slowly dying. But I must protect our child. Esmie, my servant, has been wonderful to me. I told her to give you this if something bad should happen to me. My doctor's name is Courtnay Adams at St. Joseph's Hospital. I have left instructions with her that our baby is to be released only to you, since I have no other family. I love you, my dearest. Take care of yourself and our baby.

Your ever-loving Valerie

"Valerie, Valerie," I sobbed, remembering the Job's tears. "You should have told me about the baby. Didn't I warn you about those bad-luck seeds?" Even as I spoke, I knew I was stupidly grasping at straws for something to blame.

Suddenly Esmie was at my elbow with a shot of whiskey. "Straighten yourself up, sar," she said briskly. "I jus' call cab for you. Go see your baby. We talk later."

The drive to St. Joseph's was a blur. When I arrived at the hospital, the kindly receptionist offered me a chair. "Take deep breaths, sir," she said. "It will help calm you."

"Thanks. I'd like to see Dr. Courtnay Adams," I said, managing to choke the words out.

Dr. Adams, a thin, grey-haired woman dressed in a crisp white jacket, looked professional and assured. "How may I help?" she asked, extending her hand.

"I'm Caleb Douglas, Valerie Ingram's friend," I said haltingly.

Dr. Adams leaned closer, smiling gently. "I'm so sorry about Valerie. But I'm glad to meet the baby's father."

I nodded and was grateful that she didn't register any surprise at my obvious youth.

"Your baby's fine. And in spite of a difficult delivery, she should be well enough to be released tomorrow. But because

Valerie wasn't well throughout her pregnancy, we just want to be certain before the baby goes home that she's in excellent health. I'm sure you must be anxious to see your daughter. But try to be strong. No more tears. It's not what Valerie would have wanted." The room seemed to spin, and Dr. Adams steadied me with a firm hand. "Come, let's go to the nursery," she said soothingly.

All I could think was that I had a daughter, and I wondered if I would be able to distinguish her cry from those of all the other babies. I wanted nothing more than to love and protect her always.

As we approached the tiny cribs, Dr. Adams held back for a moment. "Wait here. I'll bring her to you." Almost immediately she returned with a squawking pink baby in her arms. "Here she is. She's so beautiful.

I stood in stunned silence, unable to take my eyes off the little pink bundle that was handed to me. The baby was unbelievably soft and beautiful, and her cheeks flushed with a healthy glow. Her thatch of reddish hair brought fresh tears to my eyes, and when she snuggled in my arms, I watched as her eyes fluttered open. They were large eyes, as green as Papa's and Roberta's.

Weakened by melancholia over the next long while, I wasn't able to pick up a pencil or a brush. I stagnated and allowed the ravages of hunger to devour me. Thin as a skeleton, I walked daily along the rocky shore near our home, battered by the wind, deprived of all feeling, as if I had no eyes or senses.

When Roberta's friend, Suleika Ramsaroop, stayed with us for a short visit, I was too traumatized to notice her. I crouched in the background like a broken piece of bracken and took no note of her leaving. I never even noticed when the cottage was renovated to modernize our existence.

My life might have continued in that vein were it not that one afternoon, sitting by the seashore, I suddenly became aware of the wind. I felt it sharp and salty as it slapped my face, spreading long, cool fingers in my hair. I felt it sting my eyes, seemingly for the first time. The wind brought a flood of fresh tears. It was an awakening. I wondered how many months had passed, how much I had missed. Looking toward the house, I saw Mama making her way down the path. She looked strong and strangely translucent in the hard sunlight.

Without saying a word she approached and handed me my sketch pad and a few coloured pencils. I fell upon her and wept joyfully in her nutmeg-scented hair. From the house I heard the first happy cries of my daughter. Running along the path to the house, I snatched her up and held her tightly in my arms. "A daughter! A daughter! Oh, God, I have a daughter!"

The first sketch I did was of a white dove, its wings outstretched in flight against an opaque sky. And far below was the cottage the way it had been. The more I looked at the sketch, the more I realized the bird represented me. At that precise moment I knew I had to leave home to be free, or my life would forever be spent memorializing the dead.

I had to make my life a fresh canvas. I still don't know why I chose Canada as a place to start over again, but I wasn't ready to tell anyone about my plans. Months passed like shooting stars as gradually my life took on a semblance of normalcy.

Then one day, returning home from a particularly tiring day of painting seascapes, I entered the house to find my sister, Sheila, staring out the window. She looked as serene as a statue of a mermaid. Her hair framed her face in beauty. Awestruck, I pulled back a step, aware of her gentleness and how delicately her hands, like flowers, moved through pockets of air as she clenched and unclenched her fingers. Beside her was a wicker cradle, and asleep in it was my child. There was such a glow between them, such an unseen loving connection, that it humbled me. I knew these two should not be parted. I decided right then that when I left the island with the baby, Sheila would have to come, too. I gazed at her for the longest time and felt inspired to somehow immortalize her. I wouldn't paint her, though. I had already done that with Roberta, and the unspeakable pain of her untimely death had affected me so deeply that I had promised never again to paint another human. Perhaps that drastic decision had stemmed from the fear of losing another person I loved, or perhaps it was my subconscious desire to allow Roberta, as she was in my painting of her, to stand alone as the pinnacle of my achievement in figure painting. To all of us, she would always be Roberta on the Beach.

*T*he baby was given a strong name, one that would fortify her for the rest of her life. The name Maureen had a powerful ring to it when whispered in the cool Jamaican dawn.

Maureen, unlike her dark-skinned aunts, was fair, with a cascade of red-gold curls. "Maureen, Maureen, loveliest in all the world" were the words her father, Caleb Douglas, often whispered into the pink shell of the fifteen-month-old baby's ear as she slept in a rustic cot by the window of their house that looked out over the sea. If the baby had opened her green eyes, she would have seen the uncultivated headland in all its majesty, and the slate-grey rocks that jutted like pointing fingers toward the sky. Had she awakened she would have tasted sea salt on her lips from the warm Caribbean.

The baby was well loved. However, no relative was more devoted than her twenty-one-year-old Aunt Sheila. Even from the beginning, Sheila took her everywhere and made herself available to the baby's every coo and cry. Maureen gave her life purpose. For although she had graduated from high school, she hadn't yet decided about her future.

On a wall beside the baby's bed hung *Roberta on the Beach*, a watercolour done by Caleb. If one didn't know the true history of the painting, it would have been easy to assume it depicted an unknown adolescent girl. However, it was an extraordinary piece of art, for one could almost feel in that seascape the hot wind, the dry white sand, and the moisture in the sea spray. There was no escaping the overriding hopelessness expressed by the girl who sat surrounded by strangers, her hands in her lap, deep in contemplation as her hair took on the reddish tinge of the painted sunlight and her eyes glinted an extraordinary green.

There was a strong family resemblance between the baby and her Aunt Roberta. Whenever the baby was held up to it, she would reach out her small fingers and tenderly touch the solitary figure of the young woman, as if she instinctively knew her aunt.

"Robt'a" was the only word the baby would gurgle in the presence of the painting.

Slim Douglas, who was not yet twenty-nine, was employed in a much sought after public-relations position in one of the major Montego Bay hotels. It was sobering to see improvements, because hardworking Slim had entered the workforce at age fourteen.

When Lorraine graduated from high school, it was thanks to Slim's efforts that she was able to find work as an apprentice to a hotel beautician. Elaine and Maggie, the youngest of the sisters, barely out of their teens, were also gainfully employed in a Montego Bay gift-and-flower shop, thanks to Slim's connections. Mary Judson, the shop owner, knew Slim from years of business dealings with the Sea Horse Hotel, where Slim had started out.

Caleb's paintings were well-known and respected in Jamaican artistic circles. Maureen had become accustomed to her father's devotion to his work, accustomed to his jars and pots of colour, his brushes, canvases, papers, and oils. But she knew that if she could get him to stop whatever he was doing, he would let her nestle her bouncing curls against his smooth cheek and hold her in his arms. Then, together, they would gaze out the tall windows, letting their eyes follow the piercing blue line of the Caribbean. "Daddy, love you," the baby would murmur before struggling to be free.

Even on grey days Caleb painted outdoors—something in the gloom attracted him. He would cock his ear to the wind and listen. He was never sure what he listened for, but he did, anyway. His eager fingers would grasp paint and brushes and, before long, he would be lost as the land and sea spoke to him gloriously in his artwork.

On one such afternoon Sheila decided to take Maureen into Montego Bay. She planned to pick up fruit, one or two household items, and perhaps something for the baby.

"Walk good, my girls," Hannah called after them as Sheila and the baby made the trek down the rocky hillside. Hannah's long black hair had become thick coils of silver. Life hadn't been easy for her, but she had faith that life for her children would turn out better, even for undecided Sheila. "Someone's watching over us all," she often said. "If only you were here to see them, George," she whispered into the emptiness that invaded the house whenever the rest of the family was away. "Ask Massa God to watch us all, the baby, too. And you know, George, sometimes I think you gone and get yourself dead just so somebody would be there to watch Roberta when she came. Did you know she was coming, George? You used to know things before their time." Then she shook her head and smiled. "Mustn't talk to myself so much. People will say I getting old."

Sheila knew Maureen would enjoy going into town, with all its bustling pushcarts, goats, donkeys, honking horns, beggars, and vendors. She thought of taking the baby to the gift shop where her younger sisters worked, but decided against it since there would be too many things there the baby might cry for. She bought a balloon from a vendor and an icicle that melted quickly down the baby's chubby hands. Then Sheila decided to make some household purchases while the baby was occupied. A crusty old black man eyed the baby's dripping icicle with disdain, and Sheila headed across the street to a narrow lane market cluttered with higglers selling fruit, vegetables, clay pots, calabashes, fifes, and whistles.

The market women called out to her, jostling for attention. "Come, darling, buy something for the baby."

"Sweetheart, a pretty girl like you should eat this nice pumpkin."

"My, my, your hair tall. Here's a blackie mango for the baby. Mi jus' wash it." Sheila accepted the small offering from this woman and, in thanks, bought bananas, oranges, and a star apple from her. While the woman was weighing the fruit, Sheila noticed a basket of small redcoat plums. Absentmindedly she popped one into her mouth. The market woman smiled. "That's a penny, ma'am."

From out of nowhere Sheila heard a deep Hispanic-sounding voice directly behind her. "Steal plums often?"

She turned around quickly and saw a stranger well over six feet tall. He appeared to be about twenty-nine or thirty, and as handsome as anyone Sheila had ever seen in movie magazines. She had certainly never seen anyone like him in Montego Bay before. His hair was straight and black and tied loosely back with a piece of cord. His eyes were dark and insinuating as a pleasant smile tickled his lips. Sheila felt faint. It was probably the crowds, she thought as she held tightly to the baby's wrist and moved into the shade of the market woman's ragged canopy.

"I'm Julio," the stranger said, joining her. "Is that your baby? What's your name?"

"No, it's not my baby," she replied quickly, paying for the fruit while the kindly market woman grinned and gave hearty thanks as though this was her first sale of the day.

"Anything for your husband?" the vendor asked hopefully.

"No thanks. Not today," Sheila said, flustered, as she tried to move casually on.

"You haven't told me your name," Julio said as he fell into step with her.

"Oh, I'm sorry. I'm Sheila."

"And do you steal plums often?"

She laughed. "No. I paid for it, plus the woman even gave me a mango for the baby."

"So whose baby is it?"

"She's my niece Maureen."

"She's very pretty."

"Thanks. She's my brother's daughter."

"So what are you doing in Montego Bay? You Jamaican?"

"Yes, I was just getting this and that."

"You look Spanish. You're very pretty, you know. I'm from Peru. Do you know Peru?"

"Not really. All I know is it's in South America."

"I make films. I'm fascinated by the variety of people here. I'm making a documentary about it. Want to see my film? Please come."

Sheila wasn't sure what to do. The young man was persuasive, not just because of his good looks, but in the way he spoke. Sincerity seemed to wash over him.

"Come," he said, "bring the baby."

Julio reached down gallantly and hoisted the baby onto his shoulders. Sheila sneaked glances at his handsome profile, all the while keeping a careful eye on the baby. Maureen was delighted. Balloon in hand, she was as excited as a child on the way to a circus.

"I make good films," Julio said. "Sometimes I film in Haiti, sometimes in Canada. I have even worked with Gabriel García Márquez in Cuba. He's a writer, and I hope to do something with the work of Mario Vargas Llosa from my country. Have you read his book *The Storyteller*?"

"No, I haven't."

"Look at this book," Julio said, reaching into a rucksack slung over his shoulder. "It's called *One Hundred Years of Solitude*. It's one of the greatest books ever written. I'll lend it to you. Read this book and tell me what you think. Here, put it in your bag."

Sheila squeezed the book into the shopping bag and shot another glance up at the baby in time to see the loose locks of Julio's healthy hair fall halfway over his face. She brushed her own thick mane back with her fingers and tried to imagine what it was like to touch Julio's hair. She hardly noticed the direction they were going as they wove in and out of streets, lanes, and alleyways until Julio stopped unexpectedly in front of a shabby store with a small hand-painted sign in the window that read: MADAME ROSARIO HERBAL HEALER.

"This is my sister's place," he said. "She can watch the baby. You live in town?"

Sheila was taken aback. She would never leave the baby with a stranger. Then, as if reading her thoughts, Julio smiled. "Don't worry. I live upstairs. The baby will be safe. Come, meet my sister."

Julio pushed the swollen wooden door open to the soft tinkle of a bell. Somehow Sheila felt she could trust him.

"¡Hola!" he shouted. The room was as dim as the grey afternoon, and Sheila was surprised at how small it was. Then a female voice answered in Spanish, and a rapid-fire barrage of the language filled the room as Julio and a scrawny woman of about forty spoke. At one glance Sheila decided that Julio's sister definitely didn't resemble him.

"This is Alvarina," Julio finally said in English. "Alvarina, this is Sheila. Alvarina will watch the baby while we see the film."

For a brief moment Sheila noticed a nervous look in the woman's eyes and wondered again about leaving the baby. But when Alvarina smiled, she handed Maureen over. The baby seemed docile, Sheila thought. The fresh air and the outing had probably tired her.

"I'll only stay a moment," Sheila insisted. "Be a good girl, Maureen. I'll be upstairs." She glanced back before leaving the room, noting the cluttered countertop of plastic bags containing various herbs, tiny bottles of healing oils, crucifixes, pictures of Our Lady, and an assortment of plastic skulls and stones.

There was a lone window, but no light filtered in. A heavy piece of crocus sacking was placed over it to block the sunlight, and a red card table was set up with two chairs, as though Alvarina expected customers at any moment.

Sheila hesitated momentarily at the foot of a small wooden staircase, but when Julio took her hand and led her upstairs, she forgot her misgivings.

"Up here is my studio and bed-sitting room," he said. "It's best to stay in cheap places. That way I save money for the film."

Sheila nodded, wrinkling her nose at the dingy airlessness of the place.

"This is it," he said. "Come sit beside me." Only then did Sheila notice the lopsided couch that perhaps opened up into a bed. In one corner of the room there was a projector and two or three film cans. "There's a screen behind the door. Let me shut it," Julio said, crossing the floor and raising clouds of dust. "Let me set up, then we can watch. You thirsty?"

Before Sheila could reply he took a swig from a half-full bottle of orange pop that had been sitting on the windowsill. Then he offered it to her.

"No thanks. I'm not thirsty," she lied, examining the thread-bare appearance of the room, which had practically no furnishings except a chest of drawers, the couch, and a stringy grey curtain as dark as the sky outside.

"Okay, everything's set up," he said. "This film will make me famous." The moment the projector started rolling, Julio slipped an arm around Sheila's shoulders. "Look," he said, "it's good, yes?"

Sheila couldn't concentrate on the images, couldn't decipher the Spanish. All she could think about was Julio's closeness.

"Kiss me," he suddenly said. "How long since you were last kissed?"

Sheila had no time to reply before his lips were on hers. At first she struggled against him, then she let herself relax under the fire of his passionate kisses as the projector whirred on. His hands were everywhere, clasping Sheila so tightly she couldn't have moved even if she wanted to.

"Stop!" she gasped weakly. "I have to take the baby home."

"Please stay. The film will be over soon."

"No, I can't. My brother will be worried."

An annoyed crease showed briefly on his forehead as he pulled away. "Okay, I'm sorry. But you must come again. How about Saturday morning at eleven? You'll want to see the end of the movie, yes?"

"Sure," Sheila replied quickly. All she could think about was escaping and taking the baby with her. She ran her hands through her thick hair and brushed off her dusty clothes.

"You're so lovely," Julio said, "and I love your ass."

Sheila blushed and raced down the staircase, afraid of going, afraid of staying. "Alvarina!" she called out sharply even before hitting the bottom step. "Is everything all right?"

"All's well," Alvarina replied, stepping in from an adjoining room where, in the dimness, Sheila glimpsed Maureen asleep in a quilted metal bed. "The baby all right. I just put her to sleep."

Sheila could hardly restrain herself from rushing into the room and collecting the baby when Julio came up softly behind her. "You like me, eh? I like you very much. I must see you soon again."

Sheila, flattered by his words, felt at odds with herself, for he was indeed charming, attractive, tempting. She had no idea where she got the strength to walk away with the baby so briskly, shopping bags swinging, her mind whirling with the memory of Julio's kisses. It wasn't until she got home that she realized she still had his book, *One Hundred Years of Solitude*.

"So the baby like the outing?" Hannah asked as Sheila set down her shopping bags on the living-room coffee table, then plopped into a wicker rocking chair, Julio's book in hand.

"She loved it," Sheila said, looking into Maureen's little face to see signs of agreement. But the baby had curled herself into a ball on the couch and her expression revealed nothing. "I got her a balloon, but it burst on the way back. That's why she's so sad."

Hannah smiled knowingly. "I never buy them. If I had a penny for every lost balloon... Some things don't last."

"Mama, did you cook dinner?" Sheila asked, hiding her eyes behind her hair, afraid that if her mother read her face, she might guess at the unusual circumstances of the afternoon.

"Tripe and beans ready in the kitchen. And I see your brother coming inside at last. So I glad it ready."

A weary Caleb flopped into a chair across from Sheila and their mother, then he leaned toward his daughter. "So how's the princess?"

"She's fine, just tired," Sheila said.

"Here, let me take her," Caleb said. "I like to feel her weight in my hands."

Hannah chuckled softly. "It was the same way with me and you children. And you going miss it when she grown."

"What are you painting, Caleb?" Sheila asked, trying to keep her voice level and act naturally. Caleb mopped his brow, and his black hair fell forward, reminding Sheila of Julio's locks. Involuntarily she inhaled sharply, then sighed.

"You okay?" Caleb asked.

"Sure."

He looked at her thoughtfully, then answered her. "I'm doing a painting of the sea and the wild birds for a man in Kingston. He's putting up a housing scheme, and they want to put an original painting in the model house. I was lucky to get the commission."

"That's great! You'll probably get good money."

"I hope so. We have bills to pay."

"Ever read this book, Caleb?" Sheila asked, producing the volume she held tightly in her white-knuckled hand.

"What is it?"

"*One Hundred Years of Solitude.* I borrowed it today."

"No, I haven't read it, but I could use that solitude to do my painting."

"So you wouldn't eat?" Hannah chuckled. "Is a good thing I make sure you eat. Come into the kitchen. Dinner ready. Lorraine and Elaine resting in their room. Slim will soon come. Is only Maggie away. She gone visiting a friend in MoBay."

Caleb chuckled as Maureen, who was now fully alert, slobbered him with wet kisses. "So what's for dinner, Mama?"

❦

Sheila had never had feelings like the ones Julio stirred in her. She had never even had a boyfriend, and she couldn't tell how often during the day her thoughts flew to the memory of Julio's kisses. A blissful smile played on her lips, and any observer would have thought it was because of the book she was reading. But *One Hundred Years of Solitude* was not an amusing story. It was a story of family courage, determination, and passion. Sheila empathized with the characters and believed her own family was just as feisty. She finished reading the novel late Friday night and was still undecided about going back to see Julio. But though she might have denied it even to herself, she couldn't wait to see him. Hot blood raced in her veins at the thought of him. She could have sworn she had wings on her feet when, on Saturday morning, she headed into Montego Bay.

It didn't take her long to find the store where Julio lived. Only this time it looked even dingier. In fact, she noticed that a family of brown spiders had taken up residence behind the glass window out front. The paint on the wooden door was more cracked than she remembered, and the hinges looked as if they were about to burst. She had taken care to wear a watch. So, realizing it was only 10:30, she figured she would kill time elsewhere when the door flew open. It was Julio. He was shirtless. Sheila's hand flew to her mouth to stifle her gasp, but there was no mistaking the smile on Julio's face.

"Saw you from the window upstairs," he said. "I'm glad you came. Come inside. You tired?"

"I'm fine," she replied, the pounding of her heart practically drowning out the sound of her voice.

Julio reached out and tenderly took her hand. "Come, my sister isn't here today. And since you don't have the baby, that's good. We have the place to ourselves."

Sheila felt a rush of excitement, and wasn't sure if she should be wary. There was no doubt about Julio's intentions as he silently closed the door behind them and bolted it from the inside.

"Good," he said. "Stand there. Let me look at you. You're so pretty." In a moment his lips were on hers, his hands groping for fastenings on her clothing. He didn't stop until she stood before him naked. Whistling with approval, he slipped out of his jeans.

Sheila stayed with him until well into the afternoon. She had no desire to eat or drink. She felt as though her whole body radiated pleasure as she and Julio lay on the musty fold-out couch. She told him that she loved him, and the film she had originally come to see was long forgotten.

❦

Sheila didn't see Julio the next day or the one after that. He was busy filming, he told her. She expected that a man as attractive as he was had lots of women in his life. She agonized over imagined things he might be doing and grew increasingly depressed. Sheila didn't see Julio again until two months later, and only by chance.

She was in Montego Bay and he was riding down Market Street on a bicycle, looking like a god with his hair flying. He saw her and waved her over, then acted as though he had only recently seen her. He never explained his absence. Sheila wanted to grab him right there on the street, but restrained herself.

He was all set to leave when he kissed her lightly on the cheek. "See you soon."

She tried to think of something to say, anything that would detain him. "I finished the book."

"Good. Like it?"

"Very much."

"See you then. Got work to do."

Sheila felt weak. He had that effect on her, yet she also wanted to pound her fists into something. It was so frustrating dealing with him.

A month later he appeared on the beach, not far from where Sheila lived. He was filming wild birds, he said, and asked her if she wanted to come to his place.

This time Alvarina was home with a client. She looked up sulkily as Sheila and Julio entered and climbed the stairs.

"Hello," Sheila called out, trying to be friendly. But Alvarina didn't reply, or else she was too busy reading tea leaves. She and the customer sat at the card table, teacups and a black potbellied teapot before them. The air was redolent with fragrant herbs.

There was something in that scent that was dense and biting, frightening and exciting. It conjured up memories of Julio and how his practised hands had pressed against her as she had stood before him that first time. Following her lover up the stairs, she thought her heart would explode with excitement, knowing she would have even more memories to savour.

It was another two months before Sheila saw Julio again. This time he told her he needed money to complete his film, otherwise he would have to leave Jamaica and return to Peru. She was devastated. She didn't even want to imagine what life would be like without him, because the times when she didn't see him were bad enough. How awful it would be if he wasn't here at all.

"How much money do you need?" she asked.

"Maybe a thousand dollars. Maybe more."

"What if I could help? Would you stay?"

"Of course I'd stay. I'd have to finish the film."

Sheila, who had never worked, wondered how she could get hold of a thousand dollars. She walked through several scenarios in her mind, then arrived at the answer. Didn't she inherit money in Roberta's will? Perhaps she could use some of it, and if that wasn't possible, maybe she could ask Caleb for help. But how would she explain Julio? For the moment, though, he was in her arms and his kisses were furious.

"When do you need the money?" she asked weakly.

"In three days at least, or my project will be shut down. Fuck those damn officials!"

Sheila didn't like it when he spoke like that. She liked to think of him as an innocent, even though the way he made love to her proved he wasn't.

"How much money did I really get from Roberta?" Sheila asked Hannah cagily, Julio's lovemaking still giving her a rosy glow.

"Enough," Hannah replied. "Enough to start a career or put you through school. Thinking of going back?"

"No, Mama. I wanted to buy something."

Hannah chuckled good-naturedly. "So what you buying, sweetheart? A car?"

"It's sort of an investment."

"What you mean?"

"A friend of mine's making a film here and needs money to finish it."

"The film good? Who the friend?"

"You don't know him, Mama. His name's Julio, and from what I've seen of the film, it's bound to become famous."

"Tell me something, Sheila. Him ask you for money?"

"No...but I'd like to help him."

"You in love with him?"

"What do you mean, Mama?"

"Why you blushing? You sleeping with him?"

"Mama!"

"Tell me, Sheila."

"I love him very much."

"Well, I only hope he love you. You can't buy love. Remember that. Him nice? When I going to meet him?"

"Soon, Mama, soon."

"Hope is not too much you need."

"Only a thousand dollars."

"What?" Hannah was startled by the amount, but when she saw the pleading look on Sheila's face, she softened. "Okay, I arrange it with bank. You happy now? I only glad is not the whole thing you want. And I hope to God this man love you."

When Sheila met Julio in his studio to deliver the money, she found him strangely formal. He kissed her on the cheek and said he would never forget her kindness. Still, she felt somewhat betrayed, since she had expected him to grab her and kiss her passionately, then ravish her with love. But he did none of those things. And although it was only six o'clock on a Saturday evening and the night was young, he told her it was getting late and he had work to do. He thanked her again for the money, then saw her to the door.

"I love you, Julio," she said, hoping to at least, in this way, arouse him.

"Me, too" was all he said before closing the door.

A day or so later she was back at the shop. The Madame Rosario sign was still in the window. Sheila hesitated before pushing open the door, then gave into impulse. Alvarina was sitting at the card table, smoking a cigarette. She looked wretchedly gaunt as her red lips crooked into a smile.

"Is you, Sheila?" she said. "You come to see Julio?"

"Is your brother home?"

"Julio not my brother! What make you think him my brother?" She stubbed out the cigarette angrily. "He my lover. He have many lovers."

Sheila's stomach lurched. She grabbed hold of the card table for support, then sat down in the chair opposite Alvarina's. "Lovers? He said you're his sister."

"Julio joke," the woman said scornfully, lighting another cigarette. "He bring lots of ladies here. Spend lots of money, too. But he gone now to Hungary. Something about a film on Gypsies."

"No, Julio wouldn't go without telling me."

"See for yourself. His room empty. We make sweet love last night."

Sheila didn't want to hear any more. She felt nauseated and wanted to run away, but she had to see for herself if Alvarina was telling the truth.

Felling weak in the knees, she climbed the stairs, then almost toppled over when she found the room empty except for the old couch. Even the chest of drawers was gone. "Julio," she whispered into the dimly lit room. "I love you so much." But nothing in the darkness replied.

Alvarina was waiting for her at the bottom of the stairs, cigarette in hand. "Want him back?" she challenged. "You have to try Obeah. No woman can hold him. I know as fact."

Sheila sat down heavily at the card table, head spinning. "Tell me what to do. I love him so much."

Alvarina grinned broadly. "I know you love him, but love never enough. You have to try Obeah. Is the only thing. Give me a few coins, okay, sweetie?"

Reluctantly Sheila handed over some loose change, and Alvarina's eyes glinted with satisfaction. "You have to get an empty box. Put piece of his hair or a picture of him inside. Put a magnet in with it, but put honey on the magnet first. It will pull hungry spirits. Close the box and light a beeswax candle. Tell the spirits to ask the Lady Ezili, who their queen, to bring your man back. Then snuff out the candle. Don't blow it out. Use your flesh, or else Obeah won't help. Go try it, okay?"

"I'll try, Alvarina. I'm so lost without him."

The fortune teller smirked. "So you not lost without the money you give him?"

Sheila turned her head away so Alvarina wouldn't see her tears. "I've got to go." As she got up, the chair squealed mournfully along the wooden floor.

"Bring more money next time you come," Alvarina called after her.

❧

Sheila couldn't remember leaving the shop or how, through tears, she managed to get home, but that night she tried Alvarina's Obeah. All that came of it, however, was a sticky box with honey coating the only photo she had of Julio. She tried doing it again a few days later, just in case she hadn't done it right, but the results were the same.

One morning, after her sisters had gone to work, she found a book in Lorraine's room called *Prayers of Petition in Time of Need.* Sheila decided to employ all ten prayers. She prayed them for a week, but each time she returned to Montego Bay, Julio still wasn't there.

Alvarina sold her black candles, holy pictures of the black Virgin Mary, silver crucifixes, and small plastic key-chain skulls. Each item supplied became more expensive than the one offered before. Oil of Stay with Me, Oil of Love Me, and Oil of Never Leave Me were all on the list. It wasn't long before Sheila thought of soliciting the devil himself for help, since God seemed determined to ignore her prayers.

There were days when she asked Alvarina's permission to go upstairs and lie in the dusty room where she and Julio had lain. There, in the darkness, she fantasized he was with her again. Then she had to choke back a fresh barrage of tears when she realized he wasn't.

At home the family was aware of the changes in Sheila. Gone was the happy, carefree young girl everyone knew. In her place was a hollow-eyed, withdrawn skeleton.

"Sheila, tell me what going on," her mother implored. "I hope is not that man with the movie giving you all this trouble. At least you don't look pregnant. Thank God!"

All the while, Sheila felt herself falling deeper into depression. "I want to die," she said out loud one day, shocking herself with the force of her conviction.

"You've got to get help," Slim said, overhearing her. "Caleb and I will take you to a doctor in Kingston. I'll take time off work. Don't worry."

"I don't need a doctor, Slim. I just want to die, and if you try to take me to any doctor, I'll run away. I swear!"

Slim and Caleb were forced to watch helplessly as each day their sister resorted to another magical formula. After a year passed, Julio still hadn't returned. Sheila had grown thinner and now wore her once-lush hair tied back with string in a ratty ponytail. And her shapeless dresses barely clung to her emaciated frame.

"Take me away, dear Roberta," she whispered repeatedly as she stared for hours at the much-loved painting of her dead sister in the living room. "I can't live in this world anymore."

Elaine and Lorraine, too, were unable to help their sister. Their fears increased when Sheila started wandering aimlessly over hillsides, picking wild buttercups and daisies and singing hymns she made up herself.

"I'll live one hundred years of solitude praising you, praising you. I'll live one hundred years of solitude to spend an hour with you, my beloved," she sang mournfully.

No one could reach Sheila. She burned nine black candles beside her bed, lit crucifixes aflame, made promises to each phase of the moon, and strategically placed jasper stones throughout the house to bring Julio back. None of her efforts paid off, though. Constantly she reprimanded herself for not having gotten pregnant by him. For, if she had, she believed that child would have been an eternal memento of their love. Thinking this, she would weep inconsolably.

"Julio, Julio, Julio," she moaned day and night. She prayed that everyone would leave her alone, and finally she got her wish.

Then, one foggy morning, she got up early. A distant voice was calling. It was a voice she could hardly remember, and yet it was so familiar. She threw open her bedroom window and looked out over the sea. Sunshine was a long way off. There was no purple dawn, no pink clouds in the sky, just a rage of dark gloom. Even the lovely rockery garden was almost invisible. Sheila stuck her head out the window and called to the slanting sky.

"Sky, come save me. Take me up to where I can fly like a bird." Her heart was heavier than ever as she strained to see. And there was the voice again, sweet and familiar. "Julio?" she said, pushing herself halfway out the window. With a hand sheltering her eyes, she made out a thin grey line where the sea brushed the sky. There, riding the crest of a black wave, was a fishing boat.

To Sheila, it was all too familiar: the white sail and the slow, dreamlike motion it made as it came toward her. She saw a crusty old fisherman sitting in the prow, saw birds wheeling behind the boat in the stark early-morning sky. But there was something else. Sheila could swear she saw something glint in the nonexistent sunlight. As the boat drew closer, she realized the unusual shimmering lived in the unruly hair of a proud young girl whose unearthly, motionless stance behind the fisherman made Sheila wonder if he was even aware of his lone passenger. The girl's eyes blazed like emeralds. Drawing closer to shore, she seemed to search Sheila out, her reddish-bronze hair streaming in the hot wind. Sheila had the fright of her life, for in a rare moment of perfect lucidity she knew the flame-haired young girl, luminous in the sweltering morning, was her dead sister Roberta!

She felt faint. Her heart stopped, and she shivered in spite of the morning humidity. Bracing herself against the windowsill for support, she really opened her eyes for the first time in months. She swore at the rising wind, not knowing whether to laugh or cry when, unexpectedly, the boat veered sharply and headed back out to the open sea. Mesmerized, Sheila had no idea where she got the strength to tear herself away from the window. Her feet seemed to grow wings, for with a sudden burst of energy, like a rage for life, she raced through the silent household.

In her haste she kicked over the old burnt-down black candles beside her bed and sent the honey box with the photo flying. She charged into the gloom, and though she searched, there was no boat, not even a speck on the horizon, only the lonely wind wailing among the rocks as waves lashed the jagged shore.

And then Sheila saw her. Not Roberta, but Maureen, who had wandered out of the house while the rest of the family was still sleeping. The baby was at the very edge of the rocky overhang. Sheila's heart pounded. She was paralyzed, yet some inner strength propelled her up the awful precipice where she reached out for the fearless golden baby, enfolding her in loving arms. The sun broke through the haze, and a light breeze blew the cloud curtain aside. Maureen's bright curls picked up the golden glint from the sky. With the baby safe in her arms, Sheila leaned against the bitter rocks and cried.

"I love you, Aunt Sheila," the baby gurgled happily.

"Me, too," Sheila replied. For the first time in a long while she felt as though she were truly awake and strong. Life would go on.

Leaving Faro

*T*he moon is yellowing. I can see it caught above the arms of the ocean, even as the horizon looms in the west. Grey clouds scuttle to dance in the pink dawning sky, and the ship I am on, the *Santa Anna*, sails into its light.

The year is 1548, and I, Jacob Israel Gabay, an artist, am sixteen. I had known freedom most of my life but am now virtually a prisoner aboard this ship that heaves westward. My three brothers, Abraham, Solomon, and David, and many other young persons such as ourselves, share the same fate. We are unwilling immigrant passengers aboard this vessel and have been at sea for five weeks, having eaten nothing but dry soda bread for many days. And the water that passes our lips tastes brackish.

Crowded into dark, rat-infested rooms below deck are perhaps fifty of us. We have no way of telling exactly how many, since wooden barriers divide us. Prevented from communicating with one another by rough, vigilant seamen, we are careful not to let them hear our silent prayers. We are frightened and cold in dank quarters that reek of human sweat and excrement. We hear the wind blowing menacingly as it slaps giant waves and whistles through gaping cracks in the hold. We fear sea monsters, fierce storms, mutiny, and even savages. We also fear for family and friends left behind in our homeland, Portugal, where Sephardic Jews such as ourselves are being expelled. The country is rocked by violent upheavals; older people, well versed in the Jewish faith, are tormented, beaten, dragged, and burnt at the stake. Their worldly possessions are seized by those who carry out the law proclaimed to keep Portugal free of Jews.

Some of our people have been forcibly christened "New Christians" and are allowed to retain property rights if they forsake the Jewish faith; some do so to save their lives while practising Judaism in secret, while others choose death instead.

My brothers and I have seen families torn asunder, seen deadly blows from stones, and were grateful to God to be alive even on this despicable ship. History repeats itself, playing out the same events that occurred years ago in Spain during the Inquisition when Spanish Jews were expelled, tortured, and murdered and personal properties seized. Many of the Spanish Jews fled to North Africa and Italy, while others crossed into Portugal and sought refuge there.

My mother, Rachel, a God-fearing green-eyed Jew of Spanish descent, was not spared the spreading Portuguese violence. Unfortunately my brothers and I saw with our own frightened eyes when she was viciously raped, beaten, and left gasping in bloody, filth-smeared rags, her spirit dangling somewhere between here and heaven while we, her sons, were forcibly restrained by her attackers.

Surely my father, Isaac, must turn in his ten-year-old grave at the thought of the atrocities suffered by my mother. He was a brilliant craftsman who knew all about precious stones and their ideal settings. His talent as a jeweller rewarded him, and he gave thanks to God and instructed us in holy worship.

My brothers and I had but two days to prepare for our final departure from Portugal. I fearfully managed to conceal a few precious pieces of paper, a brush, and some pigment, while my brothers took only their dreams as we travelled far away from sleepy villages, lush olive groves, white-walled synagogues, fragrant hills, grape arbours, and our own coastal district of Faro.

"I cannot leave our mother," I told my brothers before I boarded the ship. "I must bid you all farewell and God's speed, for I must secretly remain behind to wash and dress her wounds and anoint her with olive oil and vinegar. She is so close to death that I can almost hear it speaking seductively in her ears."

"I must not die in Portugal," my mother sighed as I bent to listen to her soft breathing. "I would suffer under cruel hands here. Bury me at sea so the peace of our God can be with me. I will praise him and repeat the words of the Kaddish so that in death I can turn my head to the ocean's wall and rest."

Her heartfelt words caused my brothers and me to conspire to conceal her, in her fragility, inside the one old sea chest we were allowed to bring. It was riddled with knotholes ideal for breathing. She, as light as a featherless bird, miraculously made it aboard with us as our precious cargo, passing under the very noses of vigilantes who would sooner have seen her dead.

Four days into our journey our mother lingered between life and death: four days of concealment, four nights of keeping watch as the moon drifted overhead and the stars crouched closer. Then, with knees drawn up to her chest, she departed. And in that dark quarter of the hold we brothers risked our lives to whisper, "Mother, Mother," with the hope that God would hear and take pity on her as we, her sons, stealthily under fear of death, disposed of her remains in the angry ocean. The wind was fierce and cold, and our hearts were heavy with mourning.

My brothers and I took turns with our quick farewells. I clutched my mother's hand to my breast as I spoke. "Mother, I want you to have this red rose I painted. I will place it next to your heart, and while your eyes are closed, dream of us all. Though I can only stay with you these first few moments of your darkest night, I am the soft one who was reluctant to leave your side. Even now in this time of parting I am reluctant to water you with my tears and seal your lips with farewell kisses. You will not journey alone, dearest mother. Our father, Isaac, in his kindness will come to meet you where worlds collide in crossings. And, Mother, do not fret, for only the Kabbalah could have known of this, our far-flung futures.

"Take your rest, Mother. You have earned it. Here is another painted rose. This one is as white as the streaks in your hair, and the sails of this ship that will take your sons to foreign shores, where being Jews will once again set us apart, even as we set up altars, burn candles, and read from holy texts that will shape our lives forever. And, Mother, though we sail on and on, there is word that we are headed for the Indies. When we come in sight of land, it will be an island called Jamaica, and only God, our Father, knows what fate awaits us there."

*B*ERNADETTE DYER is a Jamaican Canadian who is a poet, play-wright, fiction writer, artist, and storyteller. Her work has appeared in the *Toronto Review*, *Diva*, *Zygote*, *Wasafiri*, *Jones Ave.*, *Imelod*, *paperplates*, and *Revue Noire*. *Roberta*, her monologue for black actors, is included in the Playwrights Union of Canada's *Tellin' It Like It Is*. Her fiction has been anthologized in *Dreams and Visions* and *Next Teller*. She lives and works in Toronto.